To Ashaya

Best Wishes

Enjoy

Sadie Chapman

8/4/18

The Legend of the
HORSE

Sadie Chapman

authorHOUSE®

AuthorHouse™ UK
1663 Liberty Drive
Bloomington, IN 47403 USA
www.authorhouse.co.uk
Phone: 0800.197.4150

Published by AuthorHouse 08/09/2017

ISBN: 978-1-5246-8158-6 (sc)
ISBN: 978-1-5246-8159-3 (e)

Print information available on the last page.

Any people depicted in stock imagery provided by Thinkstock are models,
and such images are being used for illustrative purposes only.
Certain stock imagery © Thinkstock.

This book is printed on acid-free paper.

Because of the dynamic nature of the Internet, any web addresses or
links contained in this book may have changed since publication and
may no longer be valid. The views expressed in this work are solely those
of the author and do not necessarily reflect the views of the publisher,
and the publisher hereby disclaims any responsibility for them.

In the loving memory of my nan (Mabel) and my Grandad (Bill) who believed in me all those years ago and believed in Magic like me! Which inspired me to write this story...

I would like to thank my dear husband Mark for his support while I bought this book to life as well.

There was once on Earth before us Humans amazing mystical Creatures like Unicorns and Sabre Tooth Tigers.

This story is about three types of Unicorns that made the Earth as it is today and how the Horse was born

Chapter 1

THE PLAN

It all started from an idea Zeus had regarding his Magnificent Winged Horses, it began one afternoon when Zeus was having his regular walk with his favourite Steed Pegasus, Zeus began to talk about how the Dinosaurs had destroyed Earth and he needed to improve it quickly for his new project us Humans.

There was some improvement there already. But the Earth was not yet safe for humans to live happily.

The idea was this!

Zeus thought that he as loads of winged horses of all different shapes and sizes. Thanks to Pegasus being a God himself, they had magical powers.

While sitting around a beautiful river of Blues and Greens eating their Ambrosia Rice and Sweet nectar from the holy waters.

Zeus Said, "I have a challenge for you dear friend involving your beautiful herd of winged horses." I need you to choose three best Mares and Stallions out of the strongest and powerful of them all. I then want them to live on Earth, they will have jobs to do to improve it, help and protect it.

"What do you think Peg?" Pegasus shook his head and reared with delight to the challenge. He finished drinking his nectar and then flew up into the skies of Olympus looking down at all his herd and started to observe carefully. The next day he met up with Zeus again and introduced him to the three magnificent pairs that he had picked for this special task.

The winged Horses were all Strong, powerful and yet elegant, holding their heads and tails high with proudness. One by one Pegasus introduced Zeus to Wings, Shadow and Eclipse, Rose petal; Harmony and Angel, these were his faithful Steeds who had battled against the Titans in the past with him. They also had very good bloodlines from himself. These special creatures were out of this world with Gorgeous thick feathered Eagle Wings and they were pure white with soft velvet coats to touch with long wavy manes and tails, also their eyes looked like pearls and diamonds at the same time which shone brightly.

Zeus was very impressed with Pegasus's choices, he said "Well done dear friend I shall now leave you to tell them the plan. After Pegasus explained to the herd what the challenge was, they reared up with excitement. The team was then taken for a medical check, to make sure they were fit for the journey as this would change their lives forever.

That night Pegasus insisted that they all filled their tummies and drank plenty too as to get to Earth it will take two whole days to travel into another Dimension. He made sure that they had an enjoyable time, while saying their goodbyes to their friends and family, as they will never see them again here in Olympus.

As Earth was in the fifth dimension and Olympus was in the sixth.

Chapter 2

THE JOURNEY TO EARTH

The next morning Pegasus woke up all his dear Warriors and asked them if they were ready to leave their homes for good, they neighed happily. Pegasus sent them all to a special field to practice their flying abilities and strength, while checking that all their feathers were all intact, otherwise it would make it difficult to fly and too dangerous for this journey. Thankfully they all passed their final tests with flying colours, they were all very pleased with themselves. Pegasus told them that they would leave at sunrise.

It is now sunrise and Pegasus gets them altogether leading them down to a path they have not walked on for a very long time or had seen for many years. The path was called the Blue Heaven. It was stunning Shades of light to dark blue pebbles which glittered in the sunshine (So pretty)!

They began to position themselves so they could practice fluttering their wings, once their ready they walked closer to the edge of the path and jumped! Evidently, they are all keen to go and Pegasus leaps into the air gracefully, he flaps his gorgeous wings to the movement of the wind and then starts to gallop across the skies, which were pinks and blues.

The herd then jumped one by one into the sky with dignity after him. While flying in pairs Pegasus was leading them into a bright light, which then sends them through to the doorway of the fifth dimension. They finally reach it and see all these amazing planets in space. But Space itself is dark and black. The Planets light up like beacons especially Jupiter and Mars., They approach a black hole, Pegasus says they will have to go through the black hole to get to Earth. He warns them to be careful as the entrance comes right out in front of the Sun. They start to fly into this massive blackhole in the middle of nowhere, their flapping their wings as fast as they could while going through this dark, eerie and cold space. Eventually they can see some light ahead and come face to face with the most amazing ball of light they have ever come across.

The sun is this enormous ball of light which will kill anything that touches it, as it is very hot and can burn you to a crisp. Us humans would never be able to handle the heat without protection. But these Winged horses have coats and skin made of a very strong substance. But they must be careful of their wings as they are very sensitive to heat, they can be syringed quite easily. They fly carefully around the sun, as Earth is on the other side.

The Precious creatures are starting to feel tired and exhausted by now Pegasus knows this and pushes them on, He says "I know we have been flying straight for two days we are nearly there please do not give up, see how far we have come already. The Herd agrees to keep flying knowing that they are starting to feel the pain in their wings and legs Yet Pegasus pushes them on to be strong. Pegasus is the first to had flown around the sun safety. Next the winged horses sway and swirl flapping their wings as they go very near to the boiling heat as they pass the hot sun's rays. Eventually they succeed with just a few singed feathers which will fall out and grow back again in time. The winged horses are panting for air as well and sweating down their necks and legs. Pegasus was concerned and thankfully believed and hoped they would all be ok. This time he was praising his lucky stars as right in front of him was Planet Earth.

The Planet was mapped out in blues and greens all around it. Pegasus tells his friends to head straight towards Earth, by galloping downwards towards the ground. As they do the sky changes into this beautiful bright blue shades, as they are flying they can see the sea; rivers streams, woods and grass and trees, plus the countryside.

They keep galloping down towards the surface and one at a time line up to land on the ground which makes the ground shake a little. Pegasus's gallop turns into a gentle canter until he comes to a holt by bending his back legs into pause a position, which makes him stop dead. His wings are still moving very fast until they start to slow down and fold nicely to his side. Now the others are coming down as gently as they are trying to land as gracefully as their leader did. Once the winged horses are settled they shake their heads and bodies to relax and collapse to the floor. They quickly get back up as Pegasus walks over to them. "Well my friends we have made it. "Welcome to Earth your new home!" Within 10 minutes of landing they are walking around until they come across a cave. They walk in and find a place to rest, while Pegasus says a spell for the Ambrosia Rice and Nectar to appear, Plus some fresh spring water too. "My dear ones please rest and I will keep watch". As remember Pegasus may look like them but he is twice their size and is a god! His more powerful and stronger than them put together. He watches over them for days and nights.

Chapter 3

ON EARTH

The following sunny morning the winged Horses awake feeling rested and yet hungry and thirsty from their journey. Pegasus walks into the cave laying out some Ambrosia Rice on these big leaves and there was also some nectar and spring water too. "Please eat and drink to gain your strength, as this is only the beginning of your journey. You have lots more to come still"!!

Now they are all reenergized he says "my perfect specimens you have been chosen to help this planet grow and live again so humans can live here one day.

The winged horses looked at each other and smiled. They stood so proudly and gracefully shaking their heads up and down saying that they were ready for the challenge to begin.

He called the first pair Rose Petal and Shadow "you two will become the Earth Unicorns, your jobs are making sure the Earth receives plenty of water to grow beautiful plants and Trees and with your horns you will also plant and heal them as well as protect them from harm. The plants and Trees will produce the food and the oxygen to breath on this planet. It will also be a scenery purpose for peace and tranquility in years to come. As this will help you and eventually the humans to live and survive here quite nicely. But first there is a lot to be fixed and healed thanks to the Dinosaurs reign.

I am now going to take away your wings and replace them with a horn, which will help you with your daily duties and to protect you from harm. Because once you change you will not be immortal anymore, you will have 100 years of life, as this is the rules on Earth! One day you will come back and you will receive your wings. But until they will be gone from you.

You two will live in the woods, they agreed by looking at each other. They felt very different and yet galloped away together to the Forest of Hope!

He then called over to Eclipse and Harmony they both walked over to him and he did the same to them. "Your job will be to bring the Sun up and down every day and produce the weather as well. We need the sun to see clearly and to keep every creature warm due to the atmosphere. You will be classed as the Day Unicorns." They neighed and ran into the hills.

Finally, Pegasus comes to his dear old friends Wings and Angel he takes them to the mountains and shows them the land in great colour and beauty. He told them that they will be the Night Unicorns, as their jobs are special as you will be bringing the Moon to Earth and looking after the stars. As we need the Moon to cool the temperature down and make the creatures rest and the humans to reenergize for the next day to build up their strengths in the future. There are also other forest creatures here on Earth that need to hunt at night as their eyes cannot handle the brightness of the day and because their eyes are weaker than some. You will be able to fly still by producing dust from the horn's, so you can gallop across the skies when needed.

Wings and Angel neighed with happiness Pegasus says" good then I shall proceed, he says this verses in Greek and they are both watching each other bodies carefully as their wings start to shrink and disappear, they feel this unusual feeling of a soft piercing bone growing through the top of their foreheads, eventually it stops with a sharp point to it. The color of the horn is natural. They first feel strange and in a few minutes, they start to relax. "This is where your powers lay from now on use them well to help the Earth and to protect yourselves from others too.

Chapter 4

THE WINGED HORSES NOW LIVE AS UNICORNS

The next day comes Eclipse and Harmony did very well bringing the Sun to Earth by Using their horns to power it. Their horns glow and strike towards the sun which lets them take control to move it where ever they want even though they are still standing on the ground. Rose Petal and Shadow gathered some food of plants and water that they produced everyday by putting their horns to the ground which also glowed and made the plants grow and the waters purified to drink.

Wings and Angel were galloping across the sky bringing the Moon nearer to Earth to shine upon them all. The planet then would cool down as the Sun could be very hot at times to bear. Pegasus was pleased with his team, so he plans to tell them what will happen next.

A few months had passed Pegasus calls them together and says "your coats and eyes will change due to your jobs here on Earth, so please do not be afraid it will be a normal thing as you will be adjusting to the Earth living conditions, plus your powers will also strengthen in some ways and weaken in others. You also were chosen as you are my perfect bloodlines to myself and you will produce at least three generations of your kind to help regenerate the Earth and make it ready for humans to live on one day in the future when you are gone"!!

Also there will be a new creature created and born from yourselves, it will be called the HORSE! The name stands for Hope; Out Of The Ordinary; Robust; Special and Energetic. One pair of your generation will be chosen. But I cannot tell you who this will be until it happens".

Pegasus stayed with his herd for three months to make sure that they all knew their tasks and succeeded beautifully before he makes his return to Olympus.

One morning he called them all together for one last time with him being there. "I am proud of you all, it is now time for me to leave and say my goodbyes. I have some special Ambrosia, seeds and Nectar for a special time you may need soon. I will hide them in the place where we landed. But now you all must start to get used to eating the plants; fruit from the trees and drink the water from the rivers and streams. Please do not drink from the Sea as it is made of Salt and will kill you! Stay away from the beach! oh yes "you will naturally die and I will collect you and bring you home. But I have given you these horns to help you heal and to protect you from harm, so please practice among yourselves as Hades also has creatures here on Earth that can kill you, so please be prepared and I wish you all well with this Challenge So remember your horn will also be classed as a weapon as well as a wand. I will love and miss you all too as if you were my own.

I know you will make me proud! Pegasus nozzles all his dear companions and friends. Then walks away and runs as fast as he could and leaps into the air flapping his magnificent large eagle wings, they could see him getting higher and higher as he was gliding into the clouds. In minutes Pegasus was gone from sight and the Unicorns were there on Earth now alone.

They all felt sad, yet they all got together and said their farewells by cuddling each other with their necks to shoulders, then walked away from the place that they landed earlier and then all reared in sequence with a powerful neigh running off to distinct parts of the land

Chapter 5

THE UNICORNS REIGN

Ninety-one years later things had changed dramatically the Trees had grown to great heights and grew tasty fruits for the Unicorns and other creatures to eat, they had made great homes for many new birds too. But most important the Trees were now producing enough Oxygen to easily breathe. The Unicorns had created many more Rivers and Streams, so the ground was beautiful they had also grown plants that produced vegetables and grass, which was so pretty to see and tasty to eat. Earth had become an amazing place to live. Thanks to these amazing creatures that Pegasus had created many years before from his great winged horses.

Hades did have a job here himself on Earth instructed by Zeus to keep the balance of creatures and one-day humans to die at a certain age, as otherwise it would over populate and will be destroyed again.

Hades was not happy and wanted Earth for himself by trying to kill every single Unicorn off and use their horns to control Earth. He ordered his Sabre Tooth

Tigers to destroy them for good. The Sabre Tooth Tigers were very large Cats with black coats Red eyes and Red Stripes with their two long fangs which held by the most poisonous venom on Earth.

The Unicorns had defeated them all, apart from two that seem to be more intelligent from the rest and they were also Hades pets their names were Pain and Havoc. They killed everything that they could touch and even killed in cold blood.

Chapter 6

THE SURVIVAL OF THE FITTEST

Many years later Pain and Havoc had picked up all the Unicorns routines and weakness and killed them off one by one apart from four who at the time were hidden.

This is their story!!

One-night Pain and Havoc decided they wanted revenge on their clan by arranging to kill the Day Unicorns while sleeping, they killed them all apart from one who at the time was hidden in the woods. Now they thought that day would not be no more, but luckily an old one called Sunbeam was hidden. It was such a shame to see these pretty Unicorns lying dead on the ground. They once were pure white unicorns and had been exposed to the Sun's rays by working close to the pure light their coats had bleached in certain areas and changed into a light to darken blonde with a white mane and tail with a touch of blonde through them and Amber eyes, they renamed themselves the Palominos of the Sun! The leader of the herd was killed so the day had turned to night! This was the day the Sun fell into the Sea.

The Earth Unicorns had heard and felt this pain as still connected to their cousins they scampered into the grounds and the trees for protection. But they hid for so long the trees had grown around them and locked their bodies into the roots, so now they were one with the trees. Pain and Havoc thought they now can rule the Earth, as all the other creatures ran and disappeared into the forests and woods too. But a dear pair of Wolves called Max and Ash had gone to warn the Night Unicorns they were next!

Weeks later Pain and Havoc had thought they had killed all the Night Unicorns when day was up! As these big cats were clever!! But did not realize that the herds leaders were in foal and hidden up in the highest of mountains to protect and relaxed while waiting for their dear foal to be born in peace and quiet.

The wolves had reached near the mountain climbing carefully as this was seriously dangerous. Where the Night Unicorns had got there through flight!

A Mocking Bird was nearby which heard Pain and Havoc talking about that they had found out about these two Night Unicorns which they missed before and now plan to go and kill them too. But before the mocking bird could warn them, Pain killed it in one bite to its neck.

The Night Unicorns were the most powerful of them all. The sabre tooth tigers watched them day and night and noticed that the pair would not come out of the cave until it was late evening and dark, as their eyes were too sensitive to the Sunlight. Max and Ash reached the mountain and had just missed them flying into the air, so they decided to go home and hope that they will be safe.

Chapter 7

REVENGE OF THE
PALOMINOS OF THE SUN

Pain and Havoc had travelled miles and miles and eventually reached the mountain. That night they rested near by the cave were the Night Unicorns were. They saw Jecco and Moonbeam who was heavily in foal flying and galloping into the night skies. Thinking that how would they be able to catch them as now they have extra strength and power. While conjuring up a plan. What they did not realize is that there was a survivor of The Palomino (Day Unicorns) Sundance had vanished into the hot Sun and sacrificed her life to bring back the Sun to Earth again. The only way she could do that was to live inside it. She galloped with her eyes closed making a terrible cry as she was burned into an ash and became this massive great ball of light! she was reborn. Now Sundance was rearing in the Sun energizing her horn, she now was the Fire Horse of the Sun. Jecco and Moonbeam came running down into the cave as the Sun hurt their eyes as it was too bright for them as they always lived in the dark and Night!

The sabre tooth tigers watched this and noticed that the pair would not come out until late. They also would use their weakness to lure them out and kill them both. Pain and Havoc had a plan!!

Chapter 8

JECCO AND MOONBEAM THE NIGHT UNICORNS

Jecco and his pretty mare Moonbeam worked twice as hard as they were the last of their kind Because Pain and Havoc had killed their herd. Eventually Sundance was neighing in a ball of light saying that she survived and sacrificed herself and she thanked them to go and rest for the day. Jecco tells Moonbeam to finish off cleaning the clouds with her horn and Jecco started healing the Moon from the Meteorites that hit her recently. They began to gallop towards each other and they rear on their back legs with delight! These were a remarkable pair Up there in the skies looking after the Moon and stars.

Jecco was a jet black strong build stallion (like a Friesian), his horn was a stunning silver that shone when he worked at night. His hooves were silver too. His coat had a touch of blue running through his skin with soft sliver dust speckled on his body through galloping in the skies the night before, His eyes were like bright blue Topaz stones due to always working in the dark, Jecco's mane and tail was long and wavy and moved nicely together with his body movement, it flowed beautifully.

Moonbeam was jet black and yet the complete opposite to him, she was a small build with long legs and elegant arched neck with a soft chiseled face like an Arabian. When she trotted, and held her head high, her tail followed with grace to her body movement. Her eyes were also bright blue with a touch of pearl when you looked at them.

Moonbeam was the prettiest and most intelligent of all the mares, this was why Jecco picked her as his mate to carry a perfect bloodline again.

Moonbeam was also a great survivor as she was born form the original Wings and Angel who battled with the Great Pegasus himself when fighting the Titans. Now she and Jecco were the last of her kind. Moonbeam and her steed liked dancing in the sky at night the Moon would shine for them while up there. The dust would be flying around and landing on them, which lit them up like the stars!!

It was time to come down and rest Moonbeam was getting to tired to work as the foal was due very soon, Jecco ordered her to stay on the ground from now on. She started running downwards towards the cliff top and landed beautifully to the ground. The silver dust would follow her trail when moving around, as at night time it is visible., without the dust it was impossible to reach the skies. Jecco eventually followed behind her and landed loudly, cantering slowly into a nice trot before stopping still. He walked into the cave after her and they curled up together to rest and to keep warm and safe.

Jecco heard a strange noise from above it was Sundance warning him again, he got up and shook the dirt off and told Moonbeam to stay in the cave until he came back and if he did not to run away to the beach!

Havoc was crouching on the top of the cave and jumped and landed straight onto Jecco's back. The Unicorn Stallion was in a great deal of pain as this tiger had eight claws so she embedded them tightly into his sides, Jecco was neighing with pain and sadness, he was rearing up and down on the edge of the mountain. Havoc called to her mate that she was winning and he would come for Moonbeam next! He was worried and yet scared for his mare he galloped as fast as he could down the mountain with Havoc holding on for dear life, he approached ground level where he could rear again safety to try and throw Havoc off his back?

By this time Moonbeam had creep quietly out of the cave and started running down the other side of the mountain as they could only use their magic dust at night! Jecco heard her neigh with a deep cry as a fair well as now Havoc had sunk her two big fangs into his neck to keep him still. While he was still trying to shake her off his back, he could see them Pain was running after Moonbeam and he could not do nothing but pray that she and his foal would survive. Eventually Havoc seemed to be getting tired of hanging on and fell to the edge of the cliff, there she grabbed with her claws the closest piece of rock she could find.

Jecco was looking at the beautiful views of the Trees and streams and land from afar, knowing that he has enjoyed living on Earth and being a Night Unicorn all these years. The Sun was shining on his coat and he lit up like a magnificent black star. Jecco was not sure where Havoc was as he could not see greatly because the light was too strong for his eyes. She had managed to climb back up to the top again and attacked his legs, so he slipped and landed on the ground like thunder that it cracked. He got up and he charged with this head straight down so his horn was pointing towards Havoc's chest, luck was on his side as a cloud covered the sun for a few minutes for him to see her. He galloped with all his might and drove his horn right into her chest, blood was pouring all over her and his horn was covered in thick fresh and blood when he pulled his horn back out. Havoc screamed in pain and walked backwards. There she lost her balance as the rocks were falling away every time she moved, Havoc fell to the ground. She landed with massive blow. She tries to get up, still shaking due to the fall and of course for being stabbed as well, she is calling Pain her mate but gets no answer as he is over the other side of the land chasing and hunting Moonbeam.

Havoc tries to get up but cannot as she has broken her back through the tremendous fall, so she is laying there hopelessly. Jecco is covered in blood from his own wounds turns around and kicks her as hard as he could in the head, he heard her neck break. Pain now stops as Moonbeam had reached the beach.

All you heard was complete silence in the land, then Jecco neighs with victory as he starts to run back towards the beach where Moonbeam is. Jecco is wondering about his mare, he thinks is she and the foal still alive. As he heard her crying neigh earlier while battling in sorrow. Pain had heard Havoc's lasts roaring cry and ran as fast as he could to where he finds her dead, he roared so loud that all the creatures disappeared and birds flew all away. He licked her face and lied with her until night had passed to daytime again. Now he did not just want Moonbeam, he wanted to kill them both and he will revenge his mate anyway he could not holding back in the way that the kill will be done.

Chapter 9

JECCO LASTS BREATH

Jecco never reached the beach as he was too sick from the venom pouring down into his veins due to Havoc bite into his neck so he rested and called to Moonbeam that it was safe to come home to the cave. Moonbeam decides to go back to the cave to see what had happened to Jecco. She reached the cave to see that he was laying catching his breath and then luckily her horn could heal him this time. Jecco knew that was a close call and he felt that Moonbeam was scared, so they laid together for warmth and safety once again and it helped her to calm her fears. Jecco was worried more about his mare then himself.

Pain approached the cave quietly trying to prevent any sound of movement, But the stones were falling down as he walked, so he stood there ready to pounce. Jecco was now trying to rest and gain his strength from the previous fight heard a noise got to his feet still feeling sore, he licked Moonbeam and then trotted to the front of the cave with caution this time, excepting Pain to jump on him like Havoc did. This morning was a very sunny day. He could sense danger yet couldn't see it. He walked further out of the cave.

Moonbeam still laying down there feeling very tired as the young one was getting to big for her to walk around far. She was worried and afraid for Jecco and for herself knowing that their foal is making her weak. The mare could sense that this was the last time she would see her mate alive. She hoped that it was just a worried feeling, Moonbeam neighed as loud as she could to Jecco to come back into the cave and ignore the sound. But he was the Stallion of the herd and had to protect his mare and foal, so ignored the cry!

He went further out of the cave when the sun was in his eyes for a spilt second so Pain took the advantage of this and pounced on his back. Digging his claws and fangs straight into Jeccos neck as deep as he could go, Jecco neighed with great agony! Pain was now holding on for dear life, he dug his claws into the brave Night Unicorn's side, blood is pouring out of everywhere onto his stunning shiny black coat. Jecco starts to neigh with anger and rears up on his legs to throw Pain off. But Pain was twice Havoc's size and he couldn't get him off due to been weak still. So, with great bravery Jecco galloped down the mountain again as quickly as he could, Moonbeam heard the noises and walked slowly out of the cave to see a sorry sight of her handsome steed in grief and pain and now in trouble. Moonbeam stood there knowing that she could not help him this time, as she couldn't afford herself getting hurt either.

She neighs to him with a sorrow in her voice, tears rolling down her face that started to fall onto her body as well. Being really scared she knew this was the best chance to get away and protect her foal from this beast. Leaving her beloved in this terrible way to defend himself this time on his own was heartbreaking for her. But she knew that she had no choice and knew this foal was extra special from her gut instinct. Moonbeam starts to walk away as she approaches the bottom of the mountain.

Jecco hears her cry and looks up to see his dear mare walking away, which he knew in his heart she did not want to but she had no choice then to save their foal from harm's way. Jecco drops his head with sadness as that was their goodbye to each other. Moonbeam turns around one more time to see that Pain was getting the better of her steed. This was the chance that Pain wanted as this time he sunk his teeth deeper into the stallion's neck near the wind pipe and he was in shock and started to grasp for breath Pain was suffocating him, deep red thick blood was pouring out of Jecco's neck as it hit the artery vein, it started to squirt everywhere. Jecco being a powerful unicorn never gave up and still tried to throw Pain off his back one last time. The unicorn would not let this Sabre tooth Tiger take him easily without a fight. Jecco was bucking continuously but with no luck as the more he tried to knock Pain off the further he sunk his fangs into his neck, he was in great pain and starting to feel very weak. The blood now flowing all down his front legs.

Jecco had an idea and hoped it would work! He fell to his side and rolled over trying to get Pain too release his fangs and fall off. He did this with such a blow that he broke his neck as he did. All the birds and animals went quiet as they too were afraid of what will come next. As they felt that something sad was happening not far away from where they all lived. The birds and creatures all scampered to their homes for safety.

Jecco and Pain were both laying on the ground. The stallion was fighting for his breath and Pain feeling really hurt with possibly a few broken ribs got up first. The Night Unicorn knew he was defeated, yet he still would not give in by rolling over side to side he tried to force himself to get back up on his feet. But his wounds were to deep and the more he moved the more blood he lost and felt weaker than before. Jecco started to feel cold inside and exhausted with fear in his eyes. He starts to feel that his breathing was getting harder and slower at the same time. He was thinking of Moonbeam and his foal of what sex the foal will be. When Pain jumped on him again with a mighty crunch sinking again his fangs straight into Jecco jugular, The Unicorn knew he was beaten he started to feel tired with blood pouring all over the floor now into a massive puddle, blood was also pouring out his nose and mouth too. Minutes later Jecco gave a sad sigh and took his last breath, which became nothing. his eyes started to fade into a grey colour then he closed them. Jecco was there on the ground dead to the world. Pain was struggling as he too was hurt badly. But will healed in time thanks to Hades magic.

Pain gave out a battling roar of victory. All the animals and Birds had come together as they knew then that Pain had beaten the strongest and most powerful unicorn there on Earth. But they also knew that he probably would of not of been so triumph if Jecco did not battle Havoc earlier. They knew it was an unfair fight!

Pain now was the ruler of Earth! When the Earth Unicorns heard the cry of Jecco they all ran into the trees and the grounds and stayed there for good.

Chapter 10

MOONBEAM LAST OF HER KIND

Moonbeam was the last of her kind that was visible on Earth. She heard Jecco's cry of pain and defeat and waited to night fall, as she knew it will be the safest time to see her dear mate for the very last time. She saw Pain laying not far away from Jecco's body licking his paws and his wounds, looking very proud of himself as well. He later ran off into the darkness.

Moonbeam reached the stream where her faithful steed was laying still like the shell he had become. She bent over her neck to nozzle him to wake up. But he would not move and when she felt his touch he was stone cold! The mare licked his face and his wounds hoping that she could heal him with her powers. She then remembered what Pegasus had said in the past about that if they are killed like any other creature that would be their end, as this was the cycle of life. Tears poured out her eyes like a flowing river with heartache. Moonbeam tried again by putting her horn onto his body which lit up and yet did nothing to help. A few minutes later Jecco's horn fell off his forehead to the ground, it turned soft and so she thought she would taste it to see if she could still feel him through this experience, the horn tasted sweet and she felt then she had to eat it all. By doing this not only did she feel that Jecco was with her, she also gained his strength and powers too. She grew bigger and border in body. She also felt overwhelmed yet happy and sad at the same time. Moonbeam felt that Jecco was giving his last piece of help and love to her and their foal, knowing that she is now a single mare alone of their kind. After she had eaten the horn she felt Jecco's presence telling her she must survive no matter what the cost is! Moonbeam sighed and neighed sadly which the birds heard and flew to the ground in front of her, all the creatures came out of the forest the Foxes; Badgers and bears all came and sat round them.

The mare lay gently down beside the body for warmth and love, she fell asleep knowing she was safe and yet devastated that she had lost her mate for life and that she will be lonely for an eternity While she was sleeping Zeus was looking down from above from Olympus and blew a kiss from the sky. Suddenly Jeccos body started to shine as bright as a star she had ever seen, this woke Moonbeam up properly as to see that Jecco's body was dissolving into fairy dust in front of her, it started to rise towards the sky going higher and higher until it reached the night sky. She then saw an image of her steed made with this dust. It was stunning, then it was Jecco again in the flesh but once again a beautiful winged horse, but black as onyx stone. She reared with glee and then he shone so bright and neighed at Moonbeam down below and then flashed into a bright silver star that shone like a diamond, the star then rose higher with the other stars and shone the brightest out of them all. Moonbeam knew that was the way that Jecco and her will always will be together. Jecco had then also became the guardian of the horses on Earth. Zeus gave him this gift for his bravery and appreciation for what he did for him and others. He was very upset to lose him to his Brother Hades Pet Pain. He knew that he could not go against the law on Earth, so this was his way of keeping him alive in a unique way and a Spiritual way! His Star would be a symbol of Hope for when things get bad on Earth for horses and people and that Jecco's job will be to try and help if he can from a far. Zeus also knew that he could not thank Jecco enough as he was one of Pegasus's favorites as well. (He made himself a Legend on Earth) and this is how Zeus wanted to keep him alive to all. That everyone will know about him and always look up to him and learn what Courage and bravery is all about. Zeus wanted Jecco to still be there for Moonbeam and his foal, who will be born very soon now. To show them that they will never be truly alone and if they called upon him he would answer them and then when strong enough maybe also possibly see his image again. Moonbeam looked up into the sky and saw for a while Jecco flying away proudly where he belonged and happy that he will be there still for her and others in need. Moonbeam neighed towards her mate that then had changed into a star in front of her very eyes smiled with proudness and then she trotted away to get something to drink as she was very thirsty and hungry too, as that was too much for her to handle in this sensitive state

Months later, Moonbeam approached the river bank were there was beautiful shades of green of a weeping willow trees and Purple and lilac lilies floating on the current. There was dark green Grass and loads of pretty flowers around her too. As she got closer she tilted her neck and head to drink, when she saw bright orange fishes swimming around her while she was drinking, as if they gave her a nice warmth towards her, this made her feel good in herself again. But it did not last as she was saddened by losing her dear Stallion to an awful vicious beast. Knowing that she will never be able to nozzle her dear mate again, her heart was broken. Moonbeam kept drinking and while she did theses happy memories came to her as well, yet again it did not last the sadness came and attacked her once more she said to herself Jecco is GONE! This time she hears a voice telling her she must survive and be strong as she is going to give birth to an amazing foal soon. She froze and then pulled herself together and listened to the words again and this time she stopped drinking looked up and thought you are right" I must be strong our foal needs me now more than ever." She said to herself "New Beginnings my love"

She starts to cry with happiness now the fish eat her teardrops as they were sweet and good for them. She drinks again to see Jecco beside her, she is frightened and gallops off as fast as she could, as she thought it may have been one of Hades tricks to catch and kill her, as he still wanted her horn and her foal. She stops and hears a voice "Come to the Stream tonight where I am now, call my name and I will shine upon you!" Moonbeam thinks she is going mad due to what she has been through and seen recently. And ignores the voice and runs into the deepest part of the forest where her dear animal friends lived, where she felt safe and protected from harm as being pregnant she did not want to be on her own anymore.

That night she awakens and tries to fly in the sky like she has done many of times before. But the foal was making it difficult for her to fly, as it was very heavy, as she is carrying for two. She then got angry with herself battling her demons about if she did not get pregnant in the first place, her dear Jecco would have still been alive today, as she would have been able to help him in the fight, instead she had to abandon him for her and their foal's safety.

She talks to her dear forest friends about the voice and they say to her "you need to go and see him"! She then remembers the voice and thinking if it is Jecco then it would be lovely to see him or hear from him once more. That night she decides to go to the stream and calls Jecco "Jecco I need you please come to me"! The

Star from above shines on the whole land and she could see the steed's image moving around, as if he was alive in the Actual Star! He says to Moonbeam from a far "my true love and my dear friend of our kind, please don't be sad as I live in you and our SON! "You are carrying the new generation of the Unicorns and he also will be in time King of all Horses too. Be careful for you and him please". Moonbeam is in shock! As she is not only carrying Jecco's son but the king of the Unicorns/ Horses. She feels blessed and loved to be chosen for this duty. She neighs with great happiness and Sadness at the same time. Jecco then flaps his wings and winks at her by telling her that she is still strong and powerful and she could do this without him being there on Earth, He will be there for them both in Spirit instead.

He also said that he will always be watching them from afar and will always be there for them, like he once was on Earth before. "Moonbeam I will love you forever and a day and of course our Son too. Please be safe my love, please remember I will always be with you in your heart and mind. That is what matters now". His voice starts to fade and a dark cloud comes across his star and it disappears for a while the voice is gone and so is Jecco, Moonbeam calls "please do not leave me. But Jecco and the star was gone as daytime was near and the Sun started to rise.

Moonbeam neighs out loud the all her animal friends could hear her and felt her pain. She is just starting to understand her destiny now, when Pain springs out right in front of her, she rears carefully not to fall backwards due to being heavily pregnant, with fear in her eyes, the first thing she does is try to stab him with her horn and misses. Moonbeam turns around again quickly and gallops towards the beach, where the Big Cat will not follow, as they hate water!

The Mare slows down thinking she has tricked the beast and that she is safe. But she was wrong Pain was catching up to her fast, she panics and runs towards to the sea? It is a very hot day as it is Summer with all the beautiful colours glowing around her. Now she is running straight towards it with no fear. But remembering what Pegasus said about that is to could kill her! She had no choice but to go into the sea, as Pain caught up with her on the stunning yellow beach and ran and pounced right into the water because the sand was scorching hot on his paws. Moonbeam pushed herself further into the sea, knowing that now it was calm. Pain did not like the sea. But his determination to kill her was more on his mind. Poor Moonbeam was feeling very tired due to the heat burning up her body and draining her energy as well, she could only see shadows and images due to her eyes were only now used to the night. She kept squinting as the Sun was too bright for her to make sure where Pain was. Moonbeam used her ears carefully, listening to him splashing around in the sea. Pain had a good advantage now for being a Sabre Tooth Tiger they had brilliant eyesight at any time of day.

Chapter 11

MOONBEAM'S NEW BEGINNING

Moonbeam was covered in a cold sweat, she had a white foam over the top of her thighs, neck and mouth. The mare started to freight again as she could not hear or see Panic, he jumps from behind her onto her back like he did to Jecco. She tries to buck him off as hard and as quickly as she can. Somehow this ball of strength comes over her and she bucks one last time and luckily for her he falls off splashes loudly into the sea and drank some of the salt water, which he hated a lot. Pain swims right up to her neck and leaps for her jugular and misses and lands his face back into the water. He pounces right back struggling to catch his breathe. But when she thought he was giving up he tricked her to keep looking for him and jumped underneath her, this time he bit her neck and sunk his fangs into her Jugular like he did to Jecco, Moonbeam is trying to shake him off yet the more she did his teeth sunk deeper into her neck further and he was hanging on tight. It was starting to look a bloody mess her blood was starting to make the sea a deep red. Then Moonbeam knew that she was brave and would never give up, as she had to save this foal, it was her destiny. She rears up with hope in her heart and lands with a smash back into the water drowning Pain. He loses his breath once again and notices that his fangs have come away from her neck to breathe properly. Within this Moonbeam gallops further into the Ocean catching her own breath at the time. She hears a loud roar and there behind her is Pain swimming trying to catch her up. The Unicorn is starting to worry as she is getting further out to the Ocean away from the beach. She also is feeling cold because the water as reached her body and she is far away from the beating Sun's rays. Moonbeam sees a vision of a rock as Pain is still after her. She swims to it struggling to climb out with her hoofs trying to grip the surface without slipping back into the sea again, she takes a last leap and lands carefully on it. The waves at the time are starting to get rough and heavy they are throwing Pain around in the sea. He decides to turn around and head back to the beach to rest. As he can also see something that Moonbeam cannot. Within seconds later the rock begins to move and a massive big Blue whale's head comes out of the sea and squirts from its funnel straight onto Moonbeams back. She is trying to keep her balance and the whale begins to move once more and dives, she falls off and swallows the sea water herself. Moonbeam's feeling very sick and exhausted, she tries kicking her legs as she was trotting in the water, doing her best to keep her head out of it at the same time. She is beginning to get closer to the shallow part again and then see's Pain on the beach and collapsing in the sun. She is now struggling to stay above the surface, blood pouring out of her neck as she is feeling in terrible pain too because the salt water is soaking into her wounds and making them burn as she swims to the shore. Moonbeam looks at the land one last time and slips into a deep hole she shuts her eyes feeling and knowing that she is dying as she is falling to the bottom of the ocean, she loses conscious and lays at the bottom motionless and dead!

Chapter 12

NEPTUNE'S GIFT

While peacefully laying there Neptune rides over towards her in his chariot of dolphins and see's this astonishing creature at the bottom of his ocean. He feels sorry for her and realizes that also the Unicorn will be a significant use to him in loads of ways. He holds his fork which lights up, he blows bubbles at Moonbeam's face and minutes later she has woken up alive sitting at the bottom of the seabed. She starts to freak out and he tells her not too, as he has given her the power to breathe underwater for the time being. He also noticed that she was heavily pregnant and knew from there on she was no ordinary Unicorn and that the Mare needed his help! He made her deal "Moonbeam I am Neptune God of the Sea, Oceans and creatures here. I am also the brother to Zeus who you will know is friends with your winged horse god Pegasus. I will grant life again for you and your SON! But you must give me your horn in return. With this I will be able create my own Seahorses I have always wanted and be able to protect the creatures with greater strength." Moonbeam thought about this carefully, she agreed with Neptune and shook her head, making bubbles and waves as she did. Neptune smiled and touched the beautiful silver horn with his hands and seconds later it fell off her forehead. Within this happening Moonbeam felt that she was starting to rise to the surface of the sea, she gasped for fresh air and noticed that she could see the beach from miles away and that she had no more pains in her body. The pregnant mare felt alive and galloped faster and faster towards the shore. She felt more powerful than before but in a different kind of way. The mare had reached the beach shaking off all the water from her mane and tail, she noticed that all her wounds have healed. Due to the shock of what had happened recently and being dead and now alive again was too much for her to take in. Moonbeam collapsed on the Yellow sandy beach and closed her eyes and fell asleep. Later Neptune walked out of the sea and said "Moonbeam you are alive and well. You will not be a Unicorn anymore. But the first magical horse on earth, your foal will still be a Unicorn through his father. I have given you a gift that you and your foal will be able to drink my waters and eat the seaweed as well, it will help you gain your energy when low and heal you both when hurt. But remember this it will not bring you back to life if killed naturally"! The mare gets up and walks over to him and nozzles Neptune with her muzzle into his hands as an agreement. She bows to him by putting her right front leg under her chest and her left leg left straight in front of her. Neptune smiles and bows back and says "you are now the majestic horse of your unicorn kind, without your magical horn I will be able to create my own seahorses, within the time he said this to her, he put her silver horn into the sea said a verse and the horn lit up, it shone like a bright beacon in a light house. From nowhere they could see these tiny images growing in the water, first it looked like a seahorse of ours today and then their faces changed into a horse's head with front legs too. The back part had fins and a long pretty fishes tail. Neptune then said another word and they grew bigger and bigger with fish scales all over them with a proper horse head with Giles on the side of their faces, their coats changed to pure white with a touch of blue in like the ocean itself, their manes grew longer into stunning flowing waves and their eyes looked like the sea too. They now reached the size of a Jecco and in horse form they got up out of the sea and walked over to Neptune with green sticky seaweed on their backs and in the manes as well. They were magnificent to look at as their hooves were blue too. These sea horses are very special creatures as they belong to Neptune himself. They slowly walked towards Moonbeam as to them she was like a mother has of part her had given birth to them. They kneeled before her and then nuzzled her neck and face while she was still resting on the beach. Moonbeam felt so proud of yet another creation of her kind. Moonbeam had become a very special horse indeed. Neptune was standing looking around at the sea with a different view for a change, as he does not often come out and walk on the land. He called his horses by whistling through a large sea snail shell he had. The sea horses came galloping over and then slowed down to a trot to be standing in front of him. He said to them both after looking closely at them "I will call you my dear sweet girl Seespray and for you my strong boy you will be named Tidal wave! The horses looked right at Neptune and their eyes lit up even brighter than before to become like Aquamarines, they were happy accepting their names. He waited until they had calmed down and stroked their noses and patted their necks with both hands. They neighed with excitement and then trotted away together on the beach.

Neptune bent down and touched Moonbeam's side, feeling uneasy as she did not know about this god or his powers. "please do not worry dear friend all I am doing to is giving your son extra powers to be the most powerful and strongest Unicorn that ever lived here on Earth, lay still sweet one I am not going to hurt you" from that the mare laid very still. "your son will be the one that will change life as we know it and will make it a better place for Human's to live here in future to come and will create the Horse!

There was a glow from his hands onto her tummy she felt an amazing force move inside her stomach. It grew a little larger due to the movement the foal was making. She could see the foal's hoof sticking through her skin, she was astounded. The foal was getting more active every day now, Neptune said another week and he will be ready to be born Moonbeam. The mare looked at him and smiled with her eyes and neighed with glee. Neptune knew that Moonbeam was worried that Pain would come back and kill them both, so he decided to put around her an invisible air bubble to protect her until the foal was going to be born." You will be safe now, rest dear one I shall see you soon. Moonbeam just laid there watching Neptune call his seahorses back and jumped on them and rode into the sea, "Farewell" he said.

Chapter 13

MOONBEAMS BIRTH

Moonbeam felt safe and relaxed for the first time since Jecco's passing. She slept for days and nights regaining her strength and energy.

The pregnant mare decided that it was not practical to stay on the beach as it was hot, so she trotted to the woods to rest. Later that day she woke up to the gorgeous sunshine feeling special that she could even run faster than ever before even though she was heavily in foal. Moonbeam was happy to be alive and free again. She noticed while she was walking around that the Earth Unicorns had been very busy because all the flowers and trees were in bloom and on the ground also was a beautiful sight of loads different shades and colours as it was summer once more. The birds were singing her praise as they knew that she was still alive and well. She then remembered that her son will be born shortly. The mare found a cave where she and Jecco stayed a few times before. She walked through where the others of her kind used to graze. But this time all she heard was complete silence., she then trotted away thinking and knowing that she now was the last Night Unicorn. While Moonbeam was walking she reached their regular stream where she first saw that she looked different and that all her wounds have just healed and disappeared as if they were never happened. The mare felt good but also strange as well. She thought how is this possible, then she thought of Neptune saving her again she looked back into the stream and paid great attention to herself, she noticed that she has changed a great deal. She was now bigger and broader than before. The black mare wondered if she would change back to her original self after the foal was born. While Moonbeam was staring at herself closely she looked at her whole body and noticed again that her feathered legs were gone and that her eyes were an unusual color for her kind, they were deep brown with a black pupil in the middle, whereas before her eyes were a pearly blue that glistened like diamonds. With these eyes, she could see better in the day and night too. She thought that they were great as no more squinting and causing her headaches while walking around in the daytime. The mystical mare kept wondering about what would happen to her foal if she had died that day in the Ocean? and what kind of creature is she now. Because she was not a Unicorn and had no powers from her horn as she did not have one anymore. She was spooked by her own appearance that she ran away from her reflection for days. She also kept freaking out thinking how could she now protect her foal without magic and her horn? The mare did not look or seem special at this moment. But she remembered that she was not alone in this world and that she was carrying her and Jecco's son! She smiled and said to herself I may be different now but I am still Moonbeam Jecco's Mare and mother to his son. Yet again she rose with proudness knowing that she had been chosen to be the mother of the King of Unicorns and Horses one day. She was carrying this special Unicorn inside of her and realized that she could still teach the Unicorn ways of Love, healing and protecting as well as his duties as a Night Unicorn too.

This was her destiny that kept her from feeling pain and sorrow from losing all her family and mate. To relax she found a nice green area where her and Jecco used to lay and rest before they prepared to work at night. She falls straight onto her knees and then onto her body slowly curling herself up with her neck to her stomach. She lays there peacefully for a while and then the foal kicks her stomach hard in a reaction that he is nearly ready to be born. Now she is thinking more positive and looking forward to meeting her baby soon. Moonbeam wakes to a breezy morning the birds are tweeting in the trees above her. She gets carefully up because she is getting big and very heavy because the foal is laying more on one side of her body these days. She gallops to the forest of Dreams where she approaches dragon flies buzzing around her. She decides that she would like to play with them and tries to catch them, but they are too fast for her. She neighs with delight and a fair defeat this time round, as her baby was more important than winning a race. Moonbeam is very Hungary as the foal takes a lot out of her so she remembered what her parents told her about the special food hidden away for a vital time. She goes to the field of corn that Pegasus had left them for emergencies. She was also instructed to only to use it if desperate, well she thought this was one of them times. She knew that she would never be a Night Unicorn or Ever in her death be a winged horse again.

She finds the field of golden corn and knocks on the ground three times the ground gives away and in there is some special food and drink. The black mare picks it up and carries it all back to the woods where she is living at that time. She goes an unusual way back home and walks by a large Oak tree, she thinks that she sees a unicorn's head sticking out of it. Then a voice from the tree calls her name! Moonbeam turns around to see the tree has eyes. She could not believe what she saw. But she knew from the face it was her cousin the stallion leader of the Earth Unicorns Truth. She was so happy to see him as she knew then that she was not the last and that she now could talk to him for advice and help and possibly safety while she was excepting her foal. Truth said" are you the last of our kind and what happened to everyone?" She tells Truth what had happened and they felt very sad that they lost all the families to these terrible beasts that belonged to Hades. Moonbeam offers to share the food and drink with her cousin and through this he could pop his head out of the bark for a short while due to the seeds touching his tree. The mare asked Truth if he could come out of the tree like he used to? He told her No as it has been long and that the trees roots have grown between his body and legs, which stops him from escaping it. Truth was a 1st generation like her and was an old friend of a Moonbeams before all Sabre Tigers killed all their kind off. The other Earth Unicorns hid in the ground and trees for protection from them. But now they are one with it all. Truth's kind would of look after the trees, plants rivers and streams. They use the magic from their horns to produce the plants and trees to grow their leaves and fruits and vegetables to eat, plus they also purify the water with their horns as well. Moonbeam lays next to Truths tree for hours talking to him about their memories of their pasts and of fun the they have had together when they were younger. That night the foal was fidgeting more than usual. The pregnant mare felt that it was time to go to the beach, as she was in terrible pain and discomfort. She told Truth how she was feeling and he understood, they said their goodbyes for now and she ran as fast she could to the beach.

A week had passed already and it was night when the foal was making her feel uncomfortable and uneasy, Moonbeam got up with a struggle as the foal was getting very heavy now and moved down further to her back. She walked slowly down towards the rocks to get closer to the water to keep herself cool as it was Summer and the Sun was very hot with stunning blue skies. The birds were flying above keeping an eye has they did. Again. She was so tired, she fell back to sleep. Hours had passed Moonbeam was starting to fidget around on the sand, groaning as she was tossing over. She could not get up now as the foal was getting ready to be born soon, so she laid still and hoped she and the foal will be ok. A few more hours had gone by when Moonbeam started to feel contractions. But the Special Mare realized she was too exhausted to push him out because of what she has been put through recently. Poor Moonbeam neighed and neighed in pain and was very worried about her foal inside of her. If she does not give birth to the foal soon it could suffocate.

Eventually Neptune hears her cry from the waves of the sea. The Sea horses came galloping out of the sea once more with Neptune between them. They walked slowly up towards her and could see that she was having major trouble giving birth." Neptune stroked her head and said your both going be ok" He then touched her forehead, she fell into a very deep sleep feeling no pain or knowing nothing about what will happen next. Neptune had put Moonbeam into a nice trance making her think of all her great memories of running in the night skies with Jecco when they were younger to relax her. Next in her dream she was running on the beach with him and she stares at herself in the water and notices that she has no more horn. But a beautiful white star on her forehead, this was a symbol of where she originally came from Zeus's amazing winged horses blood lines. The Star was here now to prove that she was chosen and always will be special and to remember who she really is. Moonbeam will not have the power to fly no more as she has no horn to produce the magic dust! In her dream, she sees a vision of her foal and smiles with a soft neigh, which meant I will always love you and protect you., I know this is my destiny now and then goes quiet.

It is July 11th Moonbeam is laying helpless on the beach front, Neptune calls his steed to his side to assist him, as he noticed earlier that Moonbeam was having problems pushing. He gently puts his hand inside her his able to touch the foal and feel that he was struck because the mares tubes were too small to push the foal out on her own. Neptune whispered in Moonbeams ear" trust me dear one you will not feel a thing. He then reaches for his fork and shakes it into a sharp knife, he sterilizes it in the sea and touches her stomach with it. She does not flinch so he begins, Neptune first finds out exactly where the foal is before by putting his hands flat and moving gently on her stomach to feel where the head and legs are as well. They still both have strong heart beats so he continues to open her up. Neptune cuts into Moonbeam's stomach first the top layer of skin, then the muscles, blood starts to seep on the skin and then he cuts further into her stomach where he must be careful because of all her organs. He pushes the kidneys and the stomach to the side and sees the placenta. He pulls that out and then sees the foal laying between it, he pulls the foal as hard as he could from Moonbeams bloody body and breaks open the bag for the foal to breathe the air. The Sea god lays the foal near his mum for a while and he continues to put his mother back to together again. Neptune says "Welcome little one to Earth you will be an important foal and unicorn when you grow up. One day you will eventually create the Horse!

But now relax here next to your mother while I attend to her. Neptune cuts the umbilical cord and cuts out the placenta properly and then begins to put the mare's organs back and starts to seal her up gradually, just to make sure she heals properly both sea horses are carrying seas shells of salt water and Neptune throws this onto the Moonbeams stomach quick as a flash the wound is healing quickly. The Sea God says to the foal "your mother will need you now.

Neptune disappears back into the ocean, he had left her some fish to eat for when she wakes to build her strength and health back. The foal will have to wait until its mother wakes before latching onto her for milk. He was ok for a while as he had some milk form a mother dolphin earlier that Neptune gave him. luckily for him he can drink it! The foal gets up slowly on this scorching day, his coat is starting to dry out now as earlier he looked dark and Neptune throw Salt water onto him as well. He wanted to get up on his long thin legs, he kept trying as he was shaky at first. But a few hours later he did it and started to walk around the beach. The little prince was a cute White Unicorn with blue eyes and a little silver horn just poking out his forehead, he also had a soft length of hair growing from his chin too, which represents him as a special male to his herd.

The foal decides he wants to have a little wonder on his own while his mother is still resting. Moonbeam wakes up half hour later and she feels no baby in her stomach also feels light in her stomach too, she licks it and notices that there is no movement anymore. She panics thinking the worst that she had lost the foal and Neptune had taken it away before she could see it to prevent her any upset. She falls back to sleep as she is still exhausted and hoped she was still dreaming. It was a cooler day and the sea was calm, Moonbeam wakes up properly at last, feeling a warmth near her to see for the first time her stunning white foal lying beside her all snuggled up with his head tucked into her stomach.

The next day Moonbeam takes the pure white foal to meet her friends the wolves and her forest friends that helped when Jecco died. They walked for hours in the beautiful sunlight. But walking near the magnificent trees of Oak and Elder to keep her foal in the shade. She reached the forest of dreams and the Unicorn foal felt tired so he laid on the nice soft green grass. A rabbit was the first to pop out of its barrow and come over to sniff the foal, as all the forest animals remember the original unicorns were white. They knew then this was a precious unicorn foal as he was the first to be born of this color on Earth. The sweet foal looked at the rabbit hopping over to see him. He felt calm, the rabbit was a brown doe called safrene "welcome young prince of Unicorns and sniffed his muzzle and she bowed her head in front of him. The foal nuzzled her but accidently knocking her away with his strength. "I am sorry I did not mean to scare, you please sit with me. Once Safrene knew it was safe, she thumped the ground as hard as she could with her back foot to tell all the other forest animals it was ok and to come and say hello to Moonbeams foal. Within a few minutes there were foxes' badgers; frogs; mice and ducks and all several types of birds all sitting in the Oak tree where the foal was standing in the sunshine. Moonbeam neighed while shaking her head up and down with delight that all her friends were pleased to see and meet her baby. The other forest animals scarped as they heard the wolves howl in the distance. Later that evening Moonbeam's close friends the wolves had come to meet Moonbeam's foal too. They both ran as fast they could towards Moonbeam barking with joy to see her, she neighed with a soft tone while greeting them. They nuzzled each other and the wolves licked her face. Moonbeam then called over her foal to meet her friends. The Unicorn foal felt a little scared and unsure at first. But Moonbeam told him not to be afraid. He pulled himself up carefully and walked towards them with pride. They looked at him with shock as they excepted to see a black foal like her and Jecco.

The Wolves said "why he is White? and Moonbeam answered "This is my son SEEQUEST prince of all Unicorns and animals here on Earth. He is pure white as he is a reminder of our ancestors before us and to also be of pure heart and peace and tranquility that he stands for. Maybe in time he may change to our color, no one knows? The wolves respected the mare's answer and went over and bowed in front of the foal. The foal heard is name from his mother for the first time that day. He loved her saying his name with proudness. He walked closer to wolves showing no fear now and they sniffed him, eventually he neighed and they all ran off together for some fun. Later that day Seequest asked his mother why is she close to these two wolves? She told him that she saved their cubs and Den when she was younger and the wolves become so grateful they become great friends from it. She told him of how the Wolves (Max and Ash) helped her when she was pregnant with him being all alone in the world. Than the Prince said "why was you alone mother? Wasn't dad with you by your side for my birth? This bought sadness to Moonbeam's heart and she had to change the subject quickly as it hurt too much to talk about yet. "Come on son lets enjoy the sunshine and they galloped further into the forest and grazed for a while eating apples and drinking fresh water from the blue clear stream. The Wolves followed beside them and they fell asleep next to each other. Moonbeam fed Seequest his milk and then both rested for the afternoon. Later that evening when it was getting darker the group decided that they had to part so the wolves said goodbye and then remembered what her foal asked earlier, instead of just telling him, she wanted to show him. She woke the Prince up and said come along I have something to show and tell you about your father!! Straight away Seequest was up and excited thinking he was going to meet him alive and in the flesh. Poor Moonbeam felt ripped apart on the inside and yet needed to keep strong for a little longer.

Chapter 14

JECCO THE MIGHTY NIGHT UNICORN THAT EVER LIVED ON EARTH

Moonbeam says "I am going to take you further into the deeper part of the forest where we used to live it is called "The Forest of Dreams, they reached the place and walked further up a mountain to amazing views of all the lands, there on the left was a massive cave that went on forever, it was magic! Both walked in and it lit up all on its own as it had a magic spell on it. As Jecco and Moonbeam together with their horns in the past created it. They also made a spell to light a fire by throwing hay or wood in the middle of the ground. Moonbeam started having flash backs of her days here with Jecco until his death. She then said, "come on we must go now" One day I will bring you back here when you are older. But for now, it is not safe and you are too young to be even producing magic yet?

While walking back down the mountain again Moonbeam told Seequest everything about how she became a Night Unicorn and her duties. She explained a little of what happened to his father as well. Seequest would not believe that his father was dead and ran away as fast as he could through shock. Moonbeam galloped as fast as she could, but could not keep up with him not even now when he was angry and on a mission.

He cried "leave me alone". Eventually she caught up with him and walked towards another forest called the Mysterious woods! There Seequest felt that is horn was sparking and itchy shaking his head up and down not believing what his mother told him. He felt the urge to rub his horn up and down this tree, which he does and there on the branches start to bud pretty peach flowers. He is upset with his mother, so runs away again deeper and deeper into the woods on his own. Moonbeam asks him to stop, he won't and runs faster than before. Moonbeam gave up trying to chase him realizing that her sons has already got some powerful abilities where he is getting stronger every day. Moonbeam is feeling lost knowing that she has no horn to have these amazing powers herself still. His mother gives up and slows herself down to lay next to tree after all Seequest was 3 months old and needed to start to defend himself. She knew he would be back as he will need her for at least another six months. There was a beautiful bright full moon, the moon shone on her stunning black coat where it still lit up with a touch of blue sparkle in it. Then she felt the moonlight shine on to her head, which made her look up in the sky and see the stars. Oh, she missed being up there with Jecco and it also made her remember about losing her dearly beloved. Tears roll down her eyes and she says, "I miss you" She fell asleep dreaming about him. She heard in the distance a heavy galloping from afar, she could not believe her eyes that within the six hours that Seequest had gone away he had grown again to a six-month-old colt. She looked at him scared as she was not aware of this type of magic before, which she thought could be an illusion from Hades magic to kill her while he was still approaching her fast. He was more powerful than her and Jecco put together. Thankfully it was the son that she knew and loved, she welcomed him back by throwing her head over his back. Seequest was now nearly the size of his mother. His Silver horn had also grown too and his mane and tail had become more longer as well. Moonbeam was astounded at how quickly her foal was growing up and becoming an adult within a few months of birth. Seequest stops by pulling his back legs and hoofs into the ground with a massive thud it wakes up all the animals. Mother he says "I have been thinking about what you told me earlier. I am sorry I ran away from you, I needed to sort things in my head" I am back now to look after and protect you and my species of the Unicorn! I will become the best King of Unicorns that ever lived one day too. Moonbeam neighed in happiness and they both stand together to rest till morning. The Mysterious woods was very mysterious indeed as that is also where Truth lives. But Moonbeam thought that Seequest had enough to digest before giving him another shock. They stayed away until she knew he was older and ready.

Chapter 15

SEEQUEST MOONBEAMS SON

Six months had pasted so quickly and Seequest had grown to be 14 hands high, getting stronger and a heavier build every day. Her son also walked with such elegance and stood with an amazing outstanding stance. He also had his mother's looks and elegant neck and tail set, so he was quite handsome, as he looked like his father with Arabian face, which gave him more an elegant look to him. Moonbeam felt sad as her son had become a yearling so quickly and in another six months he will be colt (young adult male). But she was very proud of him all the same. The mare thought at one point that she really hasn't had the chance to enjoy her son as a foal as he has grown so fast, so even though she had liked being with him, she really did not get the time to enjoy it. Time was flying to quickly for her.

Moonbeam realized it was time for Seequest to meet her cousin Truth another of their kind, the last of the Earth Unicorns who could not come out from the trees without magic since she last saw him! Moonbeam says "son I need to take you to the Mysterious woods, I have

60

a cousin you need to meet of mine and your fathers!! Please Seequest follow me I need to show you something that you won't believe unless you see it for yourself. It is now dawn, there is stunning reds and oranges in the sky were specular. Every time Moonbeam looked up in the stars she began to think about her your life as it was before. But she was also proud to be chosen for this special duty. It took them one day and night to reach this forest which was miles away from where they were staying near the beach. They galloped and galloped until they were tired and stopped and drunk from the river nearby. They found some shelter near a pretty bush covered in stunning shades of pink flowers and the scent was very sweet like candy, they stood between this for warmth and protection until it was light again. They also ate the nice fresh grass as now Seequest was six months old. But looks and acts like young colt, his coat is starting to turn a different type of white, his mane is now more angled and his body was more filled out with a beautiful arched neck like his mothers. They reached the woods and there in the great Oak tree was Truth stuck in it. Moonbeam introduces Seequest to Truth so one day when he is older he will know about his destiny without been afraid of it.

That night Moonbeam looks at the stars and tells Seequest about her and his father's duties and their life as Night Unicorns on Earth.

Chapter 16

MOONBEAMS' DUTIES AS A NIGHT UNICORN AND A MOTHER

She gets up and walks over to Seequest and decides on a journey. "Come on" she says and trots off; the foal is curious and follows her in the night! They finally reach the spot where she and Jecco used to work the skies. The sky lights up and the stars were glowing like diamonds, Seequest's horn starts to glow and his eyes changed to a bluey pearl colour, now he could see every single detail on land, sky or star. This freaked him out a little and so he starts to walk backwards. Moonbeam calls him "please calm down", she explains what their eyes can do and what she used to do as her work every night. While she spoke about her life again, she felt useless as now she had no powers to climb the stars anymore and be able to show Seequest what they actually did. The young Unicorn could see his mother was upset. He looked at her closely seeing the pain she was going through and heartache that she was feeling. Then he realized how proud and honored he was to be bought up and cared for by this amazing mare, who had been through great battles in her time and yet still lived to become the last of her kind.

He was thinking when he was older and stronger that he would hopefully fulfill his mother's dreams again. They started to gallop home when his eyes changed back to normal, they reached the beach the sun was shining. It was going to be a warm day, they ran towards the sea and started to drink its waters. It tasted salty but ever so refreshing to them, this also energized them fully. The colours of the sea were of beautiful shades of blues and greens, which was clear that you could see the small fishes swimming between their legs.

While they were drinking with astonishment Seequest jumped out of his skin, as he saw little green sea creatures with red shiny shells on their backs with funny shaped feet dragging themselves towards the Ocean through his actual legs. He jumped again and neighed loudly in fright as they were touching his actual skin. His so freaked out by this that he starts to gallop away from the beach bucking like a crazy horse as he goes. Moonbeam looks up to see that her brave Son has ran away from some dear harmless little turtle babies, who she looked after for a while as their mum had gone hunting for food.

The mare starts to laugh throwing her head as she does, Moonbeam walks over to the them and says "hello" they stopped still and she says "please don't panic I will not hurt you I am your aunty Moonbeam" within that they make a funny noise between them and start dragging themselves closer to the sea again. Moonbeam follows then to make sure the birds do not attack them." Come along my little ones your mum is excepting to see you all soon". The turtles all come together and make a line towards the sea, the mother horse keeps walking behind them until they reach the sea safety. She gallops straight out of the water as fast as she could afterwards, as she remembers what happened to her before. Moonbeam will not go no further than her knees from now on. Seequest had got over his funny five minutes and gallops straight into the sea as if he belonged there deeper and deeper he ran into it, until he disappeared. Next you could see him swimming with dolphins who had been jumping out of the sea watching them earlier. He looked back and dived in with his head first, he had changed again! His body had become part fish like Neptune's horses of the sea. He loved that the fact he produced gills near his ears and could breathe under the ocean. Seequest saw another type of life down there with Crabs and sharks and turtles and all kinds of pretty coloured fish swimming and living there, wow what a view he thought. He came back to the surface and he then decided to dive deeper this time. Seequest had become a Hippocampus. From a distance Moonbeam then sees that her son has become like Neptune's seahorses.

Moonbeam could see that her son was jumping and playing around out in the far distance with the dolphins, who then became his dear friends.

Chapter 17

SEEQUEST PRINCE OF UNICORNS

The seagulls are flying around for scraps and the fish are jumping in and out of the water with excitement Seequest had become part of them. Before he reached the shore, he dived in again. Moonbeam saw that he had a beautiful long fish tail and his mane had turned into a stunning fin shape as well with the most outstanding aqua eyes she had ever seen, his body was also covered in soft delicate scales which shone like diamonds. Because his color was white silver with Aqua blue through him too. Moonbeam falls asleep on the beach in the cool breeze. Later he decided it was time to come out and rest on land with his mother, who was still sleeping on the beach peacefully. He swims towards the beach, when his horn begins to glow again a bright light blue, he begins to change back to his normal form. The Unicorn colt starts galloping faster out of the sea, which produce unusual white shapes. It looked like he was jumping them so Neptune decides to call them waves and ripples. Next all you could hear is the waves crashing and making lots of noise was Seequest galloping back out of the sea!

Seequest then reaches the beach lines and starts to trot proudly up to his mother's side gracefully, nuzzling her to wake up from her slumber. Moonbeam wakes up to her son standing beside her with these aqua blue eyes and bright blue mane and tail. He smiles and kisses her gently, she wakes up with this wonderful feeling of love and peace in her heart, that it was very overwhelming for her at first. Then she gets up and cuddles him, showing that they have a true family bond. Seequest then says "Thank you and I will always be here for you", a tear lays in the corner of Moonbeams eye of proudness for her son.

"I am glad Neptune and I named you Seequest my dear son" As you are a gift from the gods and heavens above. Neptune helped me survive a terrible accident, which I had to surrender my horn to him and in return you and I have the power to drink the sea water to heal and give us energy. But without my horn I am now not a Night Unicorn anymore and I cannot even keep my promise to protect the stars and skies has I have no magic or dust to fly. "I am now a creature of an unusual species even though I look like you". She drops her head down with shame and sadness. She then said you are "unique to all Unicorns on Earth my son and you also now have a strong connection to the sea as well, I guess that is Neptune's gift to you. "Your name means you are strong, kind and caring with common sense and true courage. You are invincible too".

Moonbeam has tears in her eyes once more when she is telling him this. Seequest says "don't cry mother, I love you and rears up in front of her as he now has changed back to his pure white coat again with a touch of soft blue grey patches running over his back and mane and tail. His eyes also have changed back too. He also has the same color on his legs and muzzle as well. Moonbeam still looked very sad as she spoke about her days, knowing that she could never gallop the night skies anymore as she had no horn to create the fairy dust. They carry on running up and down the beach together in the sunshine having great fun together as she forgets all about it.

Chapter 18

SEEQUESTS SURPRISE

Many months had passed and now the Unicorn prince was a true colt he was ready to give back something to his mother as he felt that he had the power to do this. One night he took his mother back to that special place and said "close your eyes and believe you can fly and gallop the skies again". She did this and within time she believed. Seequest's horn starts glowing a stunning bright silver and he touched his mother's head and her body then was covered in stardust like her past. Seequest then turns into a black stallion like his father, he shone like Onyx, his eyes had changed to a bluey pearl and so did hers, as they needed them to see in the darkness and to see the stars in detail and because they are always facing the Moon face on. His coat had a touch of blue sprinkle like his fathers used to have as well. At one-point Moonbeam thought that she was looking at Jecco again and then she realized it was her son, as he had a narrow face like hers. "Mother do I look like my father now?" Moonbeam neighed and nodded her head up and down saying "yes my son you do very much" with a soft smile on her face. He looked at his mother once again seeing the magnificent mare as she was before he was born. She was spectacular her coat looked like black velvet glowing in the moonlight and her mane and tail had become more flowy too. He says to her "You are now again one of your kind a Night Unicorn"! He reared with both of his legs moving them up and down as he was standing extra tall with happiness, that he had grated his mother's wish. He touched his mother's forehead with the tip of his horn, where she now has a pretty white star in place of her horn, as a mark from the gods that she still was a night unicorn in a different way.

From his touch, she felt the magic sparks appear of a vision of her pretty silver horn she once had and her eyes glowed like moonbeams once more, that is how she got her name from the stunning presence she had and her eyes that showed pureness, honesty and true love. She looked ten years younger too. Moonbeam felt truly alive again... He shook his head and all the magic dust landed on his mother's body everywhere she was glistening like the true star that she was. His mother's eyes were showing happiness and delight once more. "Come on mother lets ride the night sky and please can you show me exactly what you and dad used to do. The Mare replies "Yes let's do this one last time on the honor of your father my dear Jecco and to be in good company with my own son is also a blessing" that she pulls her right leg under her chest and bows her head to him.

As now Moonbeams sees for the first time not her son anymore but the Prince of Unicorns. They galloped to the highest mountain called Moon Ridge, which her and his father named many years before. They approach the top when she says now "you have to be brave and jump off"!! What they did next was extraordinary as Moonbeam taught him a lot when he was younger, he is ready for this and so is she. The black mare never thought that she would have the privilege to do this again for real in her life time. For her this was a dream come true! Moonbeam ran as fast as she could towards the edge and jumped with a massive leap into the night sky and galloped as far as she could, until she reached a night cloud to stand on, next she's galloping towards the bright stars that shine like silver in the sky. She stops and spins round and says, "Son it is your turn", standing in the distance on the cliff top still, looking up at his mother speed and grace. Seequest was amazed to see his mother having fun and having the chance to be her true self once again. He felt unsure that he was going to fail and disappoint his mother. But he thought about his father and how his mother would describe him, that he felt his presence inside of him which gave him the courage to do this. As this was his first time ever to explore the night sky and be a Night Unicorn like his ancestors before which was many years ago. Seequest also trusted in his mother's philosophy. He does the same as her and reaches her in minutes.

Moonbeam says, "come on let's check the moon first, see how she is doing"? Moonbeam mentions to Seequest to keep an eye out for stars that possibly need to be repaired and to use his horn to heal them and make them whole again, as they are bashed about by the meteorites in the sky as the stars are fragments of planets from a distance that die and the star is then reborn. While they are galloping around they are making clouds and thunder as they land, which increases the rain to build up for the later seasons in the year. Moonbeam is loving the sky and the fresh air and seeing her dear friends the stars again. While galloping around in the night sky they have created these beautiful shades of pinks, blues and lilacs, you can see their horns glowing like the moon herself and their hoofs have lit up through the speed that they are doing too.

The mare starts thinking that it will be dawn soon, so she touches the moon once more and says good night my friend and the moon winks and disappears into the clouds, she calls her son and warns him that the sun will rise shortly so to start heading back to Moon Ridge. Otherwise if you don't you will be burnt to a crisp by the sun rays. Moonbeam feels the heat on her coat and again calls Seequest to run as fast as he could to the cliff before the sunrise. The Night Unicorn rears up in the Pink skies and neighs with all his mite and power, his horn glows just at the tip this time flashing it towards the sun, which slows it down so his mother can enjoy one last minute. Moonbeam is galloping and jumping as she gets closer and closer to Moon Ridge she takes one large stride and lands nicely on to the top, she had not lost her touch of a perfect landing, she neighed being pleased with herself. She then sees her son trotting down peacefully and proudly as she remembered after all he is the most powerful unicorn to ever live. He stood on a large dark cloud and took a big leap and flew over his mother and lands with a massive bang that shakes the ground, like an earthquake. Moonbeam smiles and says, "come on I need to rest", so they walk back to the cave where she and Jecco stayed while excepting him. She also knew that her pretty horn would vanish soon, so she scratched her horn towards the wood and produce a lovely warm fire that lit up the cave and kept it warm. She lied down and closed her eyes as she was exhausted, as her age was catching up on her now, Seequest came over and lied beside her like he did when he was a foal, putting his head over her back to keep her extra warm as autumn was on its way and it began to start getting colder in the evenings. Moonbeam felt at peace with herself and said" thank you my son for what you did, I can never repay you for this" While she was sleeping he said back "you already have mother by caring for me", she licked his muzzle gently and tucked her head within his side and fell fast asleep.

The morning had come and the sun was shimming brightly Moonbeam woke to find that she was able to see cleary with her dark eyes again. She noticed that her son had changed again his coat had black bits in it with a black mane and tail and black stockings too and dark patches around his eyes and muzzle. She says "your father lives in you now", Seequest replies "yes he does, I feel his presence" they both neigh and galloped down towards the grounds below to eat and drink near the stream. When they reach the bottom again she says "Seequest your father Jecco will now live in you and they head back home to the beach! They eventually reach the sea and Moonbeam starts to follow Seequest in it, where his saying please don't be scared it will not hurt you anymore I promise" She approaches the water and begins to feel safe, she knocks her hoofs into it so that it splashes all over her son and gets him soaked, which he loves. He does not change this time as he is with his mother. They are running in and out like young ones having great fun. Moonbeam licks her sons face with proudness in her eyes and runs away from him towards the shore. She trots elegantly with her neck arched and tail set high out of the water and stands on the beach looking out onto the horizon beyond. Her son comes out of the water more mature than ever before. He had then become a fully-grown stallion, his neck was a strong, solid like his fathers, his head was elegant and yet very bold looking. His legs had grown longer and his body build was heavy stock with elegant light weight trot. Seequests mane and tail was longer wavy and curly and grown in layers from short from his head to longer at his shoulders. his tail was high set like his mothers with thicker texture to it, his coat looked like pure velvet like hers before. He stood there looking up in the distance like a true stallion stood when protecting his herd, he then said its time for lunch and decided he wanted to try something different to eat, so his mother recommended these yummy berries in the woods. Later while they were standing still on the beach it was around the time the sun was at its hottest and they normally hit the shade. But this time Seequest stood there feeling the heat on his body. The hot sun was bleaching his body to a dark blonde (Palomino) and his mane and tail changed to honey white with Amber eyes that glowed like the actual sun rays. Moonbeam says, "Oh my god look at you" and her son freaks out and says, "why what's wrong with me"? He rushes to the sea and sees himself and panics and runs into the water as he does not understand what has happened to him. Moonbeam shouts over to him and reassures him that he has the power of the Day Unicorns as well now, as he has come of age to receive all the powers of his kind. Moonbeam says "I have always said before you were different to any other unicorn that has lived here on Earth and you have every power of them and more.

You are the last true Unicorn with every power known to us and your destiny is to one day bring the Horse to Earth my son!

Chapter 19

DESTINY HAS SPOKEN

Many years have passed Seequest has become a magnificent Unicorn stallion, who now can control all his powers. Everywhere he walked the flowers would grow and bloom underneath his feet once spring came back, when he drank from the streams and lakes and rivers they would glow of steel blue and stay that way as he purified it with the touch of his horn touching the water for all forest animals to drink safety yet the fish can still live and breathe in it too. He loved that he had these powers and smiled. All the forest creatures loved him to as he healed them when they were injured by Hades creatures. But he could not prevent death, as this he still had no control over as this power belonged to Hades and he had to respect the wheel of life as he knew that each animal would kill one another to survive and to keep the balance of Earths will as well.

Seequest was walking with his mother one night when she was talking to him about her memories of being a Night Unicorn and being an ancestor of the Gods Winged horses and that Pegasus was his god that he needed to respect and believe in, because if it wasn't for him they would not exist today. Moonbeam felt a twitch in her gut and it hurt, she knew this was a warning to her that her time is running out and that she must get Seequest to his full potential soon for destiny is calling him!!

Poor Moonbeam, her son is becoming an incredible Unicorn and her she is becoming old and sensitive, her coat was now a grey black through age and her mane did not flow like it used too. It just laid flat to her neck. Her star also was a dirty white as well and her muscles were starting to weaken. The sea helped energize her for a while, but for not if it used too. Moonbeam knew her time was near. The mare wasted no time and taught Seequest everything about his kind and the others and all his duties to Earth he must obey. She also told him how he will help the Earth with these Horses, that he will one day create. Moonbeam was not quite ready to tell the last bit of her destiny to Seequest, that one day she must die!! She did not want to panic him in case he feels that he will be alone and that he will go against Earth wishes and try to Save her. The special mare made dame sure that she enjoyed every minute that she had with him and her friends before it was too late.

Chapter 20

THE TIME HAS COME!

One afternoon in Autumn Moonbeam decided it was time to visit (Truth) again. She spoke to her son about him in past and what they did for the planet and how similar their powers were to their own. But the difference is that they could jump into trees and the ground and kept them safe and to protected them from Hades beasts. These unicorns were remarkable creatures too. They discussed this for hours as they trotted in the day. She later returned to where he was grazing in the sunshine in his Palomino form drinking at the stream, the birds below singing their goodbyes flying away for winter, the trees were starting to lose their leaves as they changed from pretty shades of green to reds and gold rusty colours before dying and landing on the floor under his feet. Seequest loved the sound they made crunching underneath him as they turned then to ash for new beginnings in spring.

Moonbeam said "we will meet Truth again face to face my son "with a soft voice, remember he is another like ourselves who I hold a light too, as he has helped me when I lost your father and when I was pregnant with you in my initial stages. I owe Truth a great deal and you and he have a destiny that you need to be face together again. Let's go back into The Mysterious woods and wake Truth up in his tree, as for a while they were frightened and all of them escaped into the trees and grounds that they began to grow within their roots and become entwined within them and now they are stuck in it forever since the cat's reign. They reach the middle of the forest Seequest notices that his mother has started to become out of breath, Seequest asks his mother "are you ok" she answers "yes of course I am fine", knowing really that she is becoming ill!

They approach deeper into The Mysterious woods when Moonbeam walks towards a massive big Oak tree, it's trunk is different shades of deep brown and has beautiful rusty red leaves. If you look carefully you can see Truths face sticking outside like a part of it and his horn being a branch. She calls his name and through this she sees two green eyes appear in the bark who look back at her "Hi Moonbeam long time no see, how can I help you", she answers "Truth its time" she says to him! The forest animals appear foxes, Badgers have all come out of their homes to find out what was going on. The squirrels are sitting on the trees watching from a distance too. Everyone also came to greet Moonbeam back, as they comfort her when she was pregnant and to see how Seequest had grown into his magnificent existence that they all loved and adored. All the forest animals could sense her pain and sensed that her health was getting bad as well. But somehow her love blinded Seequest seeing and knowing this. Moonbeam and her son approached the tree carefully and he put his muzzle onto the area that where Truth's head is, from this he appears properly and shakes his head with his green mane flying everywhere.

The Unicorn Prince was shocked as this was his first time he had seen his face properly as an adult, he felt a little threatened at first, with another stallion around him. The mare thought her amazing son now was powerful enough to release the Earth Unicorn from the tree, even if it was for a brief time by using his horn! As she knew that they needed Truth's help as well, to create the next line of unicorns that one day will also create the Earth Horse! Seequest could not do this without him it may not be possible for what needs to be done and for genetic purposes. But because Moonbeam and he were the first born from the original winged horses who were turned into the unicorns from the beginning who are related to Pegasus the God of all them. Moonbeam askes Seequest to come closer, standing handsome and majestic he bends down his neck towards the bark of the tree where Truth's horn is and touches it with the tip of his own. His mother just watching her remarkable son knowing things are going to change completely again and that he is ready to become King of the Unicorns and one day and of the Horse as well!

Chapter 21

TRUTH IS RELEASED

Later that day the black mare was feeling weak, she is now aging quickly inside, she knew her time on Earth is getting closer every day to ending her life on Earth. She knew that she will have to kept hiding her pain and weakness from them both until a couple of years in which then she will be getting to ninety-seven years old. She disappears for a while to rest and gain her energy back. Seequest did not seem to notice as he was still trying to get Truth out of the Oak Tree. He touches the bark again this time his horn starts to glow and throws a bright light, which now has lighted up the woods everywhere. He closed his eyes as the light was even too bright for him to bear. His horn also lite up the night sky (this magic is new to him and he has never used it before). The prince is touching the Earth Unicorn's horn Seequest begins to change to a deep brown coat with green mane and tail and hoofs with emerald eyes, he had turned into an Earth unicorn. Because he was feeding off Truth's energy. this was the last stage he has achieved every unicorn power and that he was now stronger than ever before. No one could see his body as it had blended with the trees, all you could see was his mane and eyes and of course his bright glowing green horn. He also grew bigger and become more magical. Half day had passed already, there was a big hole starting to appear in the tree where the unicorn was. You could hear that Truth was feeling excited as he was neighing with all his might wriggling around in it. You could actually see Truth's neck and shoulders as he was moving quite freely inside the Oak tree. From the inside, you could hear him kicking away the roots that are holding him there and the hole was massive now, so Truth started to edge his front legs to the surface of it and stretched out the first left front leg and then his right. Again, he kicked with all his strength and he broke a large part of the tree, as the bark and wood was softening. The Brown unicorn was getting very jumpy as he just wanted out of the tree, that had held him for years and years.

Seequest is in a trance due to this magic he is using, his standing there with his horn still touching the tree. But his horn was gradually sliding into the actual tree, which is weaken the roots to release Truth. He is nearly free, he has one piece left before he can kick it apart. The unicorn kicks from inside and then the outside as fast as he could cope with. He breaks it and it falls to the ground with a great crash. Truth throws his body weight to push himself through the hole and eventually you could see now his body appearing, another five hours have passed and Truth takes a large leap and lands outside the tree with half of it missing. Truth now feels weak and falls to the ground through exhaustion. Seequest begins to turn back to his normal size and walks backwards and collapses to the floor with a bang that shakes the ground. While he was laying there very still his coat changed to the colour he once was when he was a foal (the purest white that you had ever seen) Being completely drained of using all his energy and strength to help rescue the Earth unicorn from his prison. He closed his eyes and fell into a deep sleep. His horn also had stopped glowing and turned back to normal. The night sky was now in complete darkness again. All the forest animals had gone home before this and the nocturnal ones appeared to see that they were ok. The wise owl was sitting on top of the Oak tree watching for protection while these two unicorns were lifeless.

Chapter 22

TRUTH IS FREE FROM THE GREAT OAK TREE

It was morning the birds were singing their high graces of life the trees were swaying their branches around as it was slightly windy and chilly too. Truth was standing very proud of himself and having a good stretch, while looking around to see a great lot had changed, more trees and forest creatures live there also. This Earth Unicorn stallion was outstanding his coat was deep brown and glistened his mane and tail is a beautiful deep green with a shine to it and his eyes lit up like the pure emerald stones. This stallion was the most powerful of his kind. He kept a close eye on what was going on with nature even though he could not help on the outside, but he had been helping on the inside making sure all the plants grew properly and healthy and keeping all the trees roots from crossing each other underground. He also made sure that the soil stayed moist and yet dry for the animals to walk around without catching any diseases. Everyone loved his kind. He walks over to Seequest to check that he is ok? He touches his horn with his own to send a magic spark to wake him up from his sleep. But Seequest was not ready to arise again from this deep sleep he was in. Truth walked over to hear that he was breathing ok and his heart was beating fine again. Once he knew this he went over to the tree and pulled over some lose big branches that would hide Seequest under the foliage to keep him warm. He was also proud of this great nephew's achievements.

Moonbeam feels better these pasts few days and goes back and lays next to her son, he knows then he is not alone and that he is safe while under this magic power of sleep and that he will be fine too. She lays there until he wakes up, Truth brings them food and refreshments as he found a deep Dog leaf that could hold water for them both to drink and fed on while they are laying down by holding on to the stem as she took it from his mouth.

After Truth made sure she was and Seequest were comfortable he decides to enjoy his freedom while he gets the chance to, as he has been stuck in that tree for a very long time. The Earth unicorns became part of the trees, ground and plants, when the first of his kind died the forest it became dark and nothing would grow anymore, as they were the ones that kept its magic alive, so that's when they decided to help it by becoming part of the trees to survive from inside instead. Truth realized that if he drank the Sap from the veins of the tree that would keep himself alive and well. Yet not strong enough to release himself from it.

Truth comes back as Seequest has woken up from his long sleep Truth says while stretching his body, "rest here for a while you and your mother are safe, this is just the beginning dear cousin". "You will need to gain your strength and energy back, as you will need it to be extra strong for what your destiny has in stall for you". Within that as if Truths smooth voice seemed to relax him again to fall back to sleep, "don't worry Moonbeam he is fine". This Earth Unicorn was a smaller build to Seequest, yet a stunning specimen as well his mane and tail glowed beautifully, he could also blend in the with trees and plants as well. He nozzles moonbeams face and says" I will be back soon I need to stretch my legs and enjoy my freedom for a while". The mare nozzles back and says" I understand, go and enjoy it while you can". He trots away and looks back and gives her a soft expression on his face of happiness looking down into her eyes. He then turns around and gallops off like the wind leaving the soil dug up from his hoofs with dirt flying everywhere as he goes. He runs so fast his gone with a flash.

Moonbeam got up and shook herself down and walked to the stream to drink and to get her feeling back into her legs as she was starting to cramp for laying down too long. She thought that she should go back to beach and collect some sea water, as she wondered if that may speed the recovery of her son quicker. She tells him that she going to the beach and she would be back in a short while. She then leaves and reaches the

85

beach, it is afternoon the sun quite cool and she could see the moon rising from over the other side of the land. The sea was getting rougher due to the weather change too. So, she walked down to her favourite part of the beach, there from the ocean appeared a medium shell, she uses her hoof to tilt the shell to its side of its opening where there was a hermit crab living in it before, she fills it up with water and then picks it up with her mouth gently, it was full so she walks very slowly back to the woods with it in tack. There was just enough to help her son.

Chapter 23

SEEQUEST KING OF UNICORNS/ HORSES ONE DAY

It took her hours to reach him, as she did not want to spill a drop. She eventually reaches where Seequest is still laying peacefully in comfort laying on his side. She walks very slowly in front of him and puts the shell down near his face. "Drink my son" she says "this will help to make you become yourself again. Seequest twitches his eyes first and then sways his tail and takes a few minutes to roll onto his chest with his front legs in front of him and his back ones still curled underneath. He shakes his head and feels woozy from it and she says, "please son you need to drink this". He approaches the shell and touches it with his horn and it changes to a large clam, which was easier for him to drink form and produced more water from it. He looks at her and smiles with his eyes. She stands beside him watching, as she knows that it will be a while before his ready to get back on his feet and walk around again. She decides to lay down with him, so they can enjoy each other's company. The evening comes and the forest creatures are all resting in their homes as now they were preparing to hibernate for winter. The wise owl is still preached up on the Oak tree keeping an eye for danger and will warn them if there was by making his hooting noises in the darkness. Later Seequest properly wakes up and feels like himself again and yet stronger than before. He gradually pulls his body up onto his four legs and shakes all the lavage that Truth had put on him earlier to keep him warm and camouflaged from harm. Dust and dirt and leaves fly everywhere and the leaves look pretty while floating in air in a calm movement. From doing this you could see that Seequest was this stunning pure white stallion with feather legs only on back of them and his tail laid smooth to his body with feathered touch at the end, his coat shone so bright and his mane and tail was shining like a beautiful white sea pearl, his horn had turned to pearl with a sliver tone with eight curves on it for luck. His beard under his chin had grown a bit more too. Moonbeam noticed that after him shaking there was a few roses that grew on his mane, so pretty an Aqua blue on his right side representing his sea powers and there was a yellow rose entwined to the top of his mane near his head, that represented the Forest and plants, then there is a bright pink in the middle representing his love for everything and protection and last of all a Blue moon that falls close to his neck line which is a gift from his father above. Moonbeam says" Oh my son you are blessed and ready"! Then she sees standing in front of her the true Prince of Unicorns and King of the horse. He brushes his mother with his head and says, "is Truth Free"? "yes, my son he is gone for a while to enjoy his freedom while he can". And they then decide to go and find him.

Seequest finds Truth staring at the sea, he gallops down to him and rears up in front of him, showing his boss. Truth says, "you must go into the sea and gain your full strength and ability back, as you will be out of action for a while on a temporary basis". The prince looked at the unicorn with puzzlement in his eyes and yet understood and obeyed what he said. He galloped into the sea as far as he could go and bathed in it, eventually they could not see him, Seequest felt at home there and kicked his feet in a doggy paddle until no one could see him properly and again changed into Hippocampus (Sea horse). He met up with his dear friends the dolphins and dived with them. An hour had passed and Moonbeam and Truth were still looking out to sea, when they saw a flash of a big white head appear in the waves, as he got closer to the shore. Seequest was glowing like a star in the sky, so bright that his mother and cousin had to turn away from him. He shook the water off himself and his glow calmed down again. He said, "you can look at me now its ok." They turned around and his mother and Truth could see a difference in him that they bow down to him. As now he is ready to become the King! Seequest looked astounding, Truth knew that he was ready for the next task. His muscles had grown harder on his hinds and shoulders and neck.

He still had Aqua blue eyes that you could not see his pupil as it was too bright to focus to study them and yet there was a soft sparkle, showing his magic is charged to its full capacity. The dolphins appeared and the Sea horses were jumping out of ocean with excitement for their dear friend and how superb he had become in such a short time here on Earth. Neptune appeared out of the water knowing that he had done the right thing saving Moonbeam many years ago. He smiled and dived back into the sea.

The Night was near and the sand was becoming to cold to walk on, so they all decided to go somewhere warmer until Spring is back. Once they reached the top of the cliff which was their favourite spot for looking as far as the ocean went. Moonbeam said" You are now my Prince and bows to him. She walks backwards away from him and Truth says "Thank you for freeing me and for letting me be part of this miracle which will happen soon, he then bows with his head underneath his chest and puts his head to the ground with no eye contact. Seequests nips his mane as respect and walks pass him and then Truth follows. Once he is closer to the surface edge he neighs to his mother she turns around to see his standing up on his twos back legs facing the land, she neighs back with proudness, when he touches the ground he needs to be careful as he could crack it because of his powers. Truth then walks over to Seequest and tells him his next task is to go and find the Crystal Heart that Pegasus left their ancestors before them. "You will need to go to the north side of the land, where Hades beasts live, as Panic stole it from your father after the battle as he was the keeper of it until then. Now it's your turn to retrieve the crystal Heart of souls back to where it belongs with us". The Unicorn Prince nods his head and gallops off into the darkness.

Chapter 24

THE CRYSTAL HEART OF SOULS

Three months had passed and Moonbeam was worried about her son and remembered that he was the Prince of Unicorns and he will have to live without her one day and she begin to cry. Seequest was worried about his mother as he had noticed the change in her and he knew now that she was ill. He felt sad and yet knew he had a mission to do, so he tries to concrete on that. The Winter was bad and froze everything, now it was coming to the end as the grass had begun to grow again, Moonbeam noticed that there are little flowers appeared under her feet, she knew her son was close. That afternoon while Moonbeam is grazing on her own she hears a noise and looks up to see her son running straight towards her at full speed with something in his mouth, he is galloping so fast she is frightened that will not stop and knock her over. Eventually his gallop turns into a soft canter and then skids his back legs to stop himself and inch just away from her. The mare saw the large crystal heart sitting in his mouth quite comfortably, as he held it between his tongue and teeth and yet still could breathe properly while holding it. He drops it gently on the ground and looks at his mother and greets her with a comfort hug. Truth appears from the woods and says, "come on it is time, we must go to the golden field of corn", where Moonbeam had been before in her past.

This was the actual spot where Pegasus himself had landed nearly a century ago, no plants would grow over his steps. But they saw a pretty field of golden corn (Sweetcorn crop) everyone knew it was special and sacred too. They would only go there on special occasions. Truth tells Moonbeams' son to lay the heart in the center where Pegasus foot prints are which he does and walks away from it. The dear mare winked at her son and walked away to a near tree for shade Truth tells Seequest what will happen next will be out of this world and is an amazing miracle which will happen soon.

Truth tells the Prince that they must keep their horns touching all the time while this miracle is happening, as otherwise someone could die. They begin to approach the open space where they both are standing the opposite side of the heart where their actual horns can touch properly. They walk closer and touch their horns, the whole sky lights up and rises to the heavens above. There was a flash of light, Moonbeam is about a foot way watching as she is too weak to be part of this miracle. She seemed excited and yet scared as she knew that there will be a day that she will have to say goodbye to this world she loved so much and her son.

Not being able to see nothing or anything but complete darkness, death itself.

Seequest is now four years old and has become a stunning Unicorn stallion with all the great powers of his kind. He was ready to become the King of Unicorns and father of the horse! When Seequest and Truth are touching their horns together the crystal heart breaks. Two hours had passed and they managed to lay down, their eyes were closed again as the light was too bright, the flash of light glowed and rose from the crystal itself. When the crystal broke, there was a voice that came from it, the voice of Pegasus himself. The light flashed back onto the crystal so it was now safe to open their eyes, they saw in the crystal Pegasus's image as clear as day there was a stunning white glow of purity and peace He said, "well done my cousins, I am proud of you all". From crystal strikes a lightning bolt that lights up the sky and turns straight back to the Crystal Heart, which then bounces back onto Truth and Seequest's horns. The magic was more powerful than they have both felt ever before. They neighed loudly due to being pushed and frightened to move from the spot where they were. They felt that the magic was running through their horns and into their minds and it hurt because it then went through their bodies too. Then the ray of light goes onto both Unicorns horns again and this time aimed straight to their hearts, as this was happening the light had changed into a red, pinkish flame, an hour later had passed and the crystal heart had received both the unicorn's powers and Pegasus's too, it then flew straight into Seequests stomach. He neighs in great pain so loudly that he makes the land shake for a while, he was scared. But he would not move even though the pain was agonizing The Prince could feel something happening inside which made him feel very strange and different. It was now night time the ritual was done and completed they both opened their eyes as they again heard Pegasus voice in the stone, they looked closer as they could see moving inside was Pegasus's true image. Pegasus says" It is done, good luck my boy and disappears into the dust of the crystal heart. The stone fades and too turns into dust. From this grew a beautiful yellow rose bush representing Pegasus happiness that he saw his dear family again and doing well on Earth like he hoped. Both Unicorns are both exhausted they close their eyes once again and fall into a deep sleep. Morning came and Truth was awake first to see Pegasus's image was in the rose bush, looking towards Seequest laying down on the ground peacefully. He says, "It is his destiny now" and then vanishes.

Chapter 25

THE MIRACLE

Truth then gets up and walks over to Moonbeam and Seequest and says, "good bye" because Truth has only twelve hours left before he must go back into the Oak tree. The reason for this is Truth has a duty to look after the Earth and its living things and eventually one day he too will give birth to mother nature herself. He gallops off back into his lovely Forest called Mysterious Woods where once his true home was, so he goes to visit it to see if he collects any nice memories before the death of his herd of Earth Unicorns, oh he did miss them so!

Moonbeam gets up first and stretches carefully due to her aches and pains in her muscles and bones, she knocks her son's forehead to wake him, Seequest then askes his mother what happened yesterday? She tells him that there was a miracle put in place. Seequest then tells his mother what he saw was amazing and then he felt awkward as that moment he thought he felt twitching in his stomach, which he had never felt before and shouldn't as he is a stallion! His mother reassured him "why what is wrong with me with fear in his eyes"

"Nothing dear son your perfectly ok, your just not alone anymore", "what do you mean" he said. "Well you are now carrying two female foals inside you. One is yours and one is Truths, you are now a father"! Seequest looks at his mother with great concern and confession "I am a stallion and the Prince of Unicorns why me". She says "because you are precisely that my dear boy. You are stronger than any of us put together, this is what you were born for". "how is this possible mother"? with a scared and unsure voice. "Hush my son everything is going to be fine you are extra special as already you have all the powers of our kind and you also have the power of the sea too. The image you saw of Pegasus he is your God and ancestor of how this first began. Seequest you have been chosen to start a new generation to this Earth, Human's will call your children the Horse as it will not bear any horn or have any magical powers like us. Once the Humans have been living here a while, there will be a few sensitive humans who will carry a special gift, which let them know about us and how the horse came to Earth, only if they believe in magic of course. The Human HORSE'S name stands for HOPE, OUT OF THE ORDINARY, ROBUST; SUPREME AND ENERGETIC.

Her son falls to the floor in shock, the noise vibrates through the land once more. "You must calm down and be more careful now as you are now carry your daughters that will one day produce and be the first mothers of the horse"! "Get up now and pull yourself together as you are the Prince of Unicorns do not forget that". Within that he listened to his mother and stood up feeling proud with no fear in his eyes anymore. Neptune my dear friend will help us when the time comes for now enjoy carrying your babies, as it will go very quickly. "Why I am carrying Truths foal as well, why can't he carry it himself"? "Seequest listen you are the Prince of all and you were picked as you will be the only one to survive this. "My son you are carrying the most important creatures of this land, they will be Unicorns but their generation will be the horse in the future". Everywhere Seequest walks the flowers grew beneath his feet, the sun is shining brightly as Sundance is happy as well. All the plants begin to grow and trees start to blossom again too as Spring is back. Moonbeam sees that Seequest is starting to get bigger and the foals are developing fast. She decides instead of living in the woods, she tells him he needs to rest and to keep a low profile until it was time and he felt that he could not carry them no more. Now Seequest was feeling more protective than he had ever been before and was careful how he laid and ate and drank too, Moonbeam knew his time was getting closer to the birth of her grandchildren and yet in some way she felt strange about it. She decides it is time to walk back slowly to the beach where it all started and to Seequests favourite place he felt at home with. Her son's stomach is starting to look like it is going explode, he is walking in front her so she can grab his tail if his going too fast. Eventually they reach the beach and he gallops like a whale to the water feeling exhausted straight away as the foals were feeding on his energy and power to live. Seequest collapses onto the beach and does not move. The sea water is touching his hooves but still no movement. Straight away Moonbeam shouts "SEEQUEST"! and panics she runs into the sea and calls for help. Seequest is still laying there when some seaweed appears and Moonbeam hears Neptune telling her to feed it to him for his strength. She encourages her son to sit up and tells him to eat the seaweed which he does easily. His mother than comes closer and stands in front of his stomach saying "Son I will help you as much as I can. But my time is running out", tears pour down both of their faces. Seequest knew ages ago about his mother's health and yet did not want to believe it and knowing one day she will be gone. But Seequest thought that he could beat Hades powers and save her from him. But then he remembered what his mother said about the rules on Earth. There is a time that she was given before his birth and she had to obey the rules of life and death of Earth, she has had ninety-eight years on this planet and had seen some incredible changes and some upsetting ones too. She also told him it did not matter how much power you had their God Pegasus made these rules centuries ago as they could not be immortal on Earth. Seequest then asks his mother to come to the front of him so he could tell her something. He looks into her eyes and said" then let's not waste no precious time then". Spring was getting closer due to the lighter nights and it was a little warmer, as now it is March all the creatures of the land and sea were starting to produce offspring and he was the last of them all. Many months before Moonbeam taught him everything about being a parent and a ruler. Moonbeam had felt like she had achieved her task. Moonbeam later thought tonight's the night my son the Prince will give birth, still laying there enjoying the water at his feet and brushing against his body. The moon is rising and the sun is settling with a stunning bright red, orange sunset across the ocean and shines onto his body where the foals were laying inside. The unicorn feels that the foals are becoming more active and that they will have to come out soon as they are too big to survive in himself anymore. He moans in discomfort and great pain has the foal's hooves are kicking his insides to pieces. Moonbeam panics and runs into the water again and starts to pull her hoofs back into the sand and making a rough wave, she is calling for help with all her strength she had to give. Neptune appears riding his faithful Hippocampus (the Sea horses) they gallop through the waves as fast as they could go jumping every large wave as if it was nothing. They reached the beach and Hippocampus turn into proper horses, their fish tails turn into back legs. They look like what Seequest had become with yet a slight difference as they had white coats with a glimmer of pearl to it and Aqua blue mane and tails with Bright Aqua blue eyes and if you looked you could see the sea inside them. They were also covered in scales all over their body. They trotted right in front of Moonbeam and then gracefully swaying their wavy manes and tails as they approached Seequest to where he was laying helpless in unbearable pain! Neptune being a handsome man of blonde hair and fair skin with aqua blue eyes also like his horses, had changed from being a merman beforehand half man, half fish with scales and tail (as that's his true image) He jumps off his horses and looks at her son looking quite helpless." Now relax dear friend I am going to help you give birth to your lovely daughters, Trust me"! Seequest nods his head slowly up and down in the sand while he has his eye looking at Neptune. Neptune next puts his hand onto Seequest horn and says a verse, it begins to shine and glow like a beacon his eyes lit up to the Brighter Aqua blue that his mother had seen before. They were so bright his mother had to turn away. Neptune was pleased that he could look at them knowing that he is the god of the sea and saw peace in them. Neptune waves his hands over the prince's face and puts him into a deep sleep like a coma for a while. Moonbeam then hears no more crying from her son and turns back and looks Neptune in the eyes. He says" please do not worry he will not feel a thing, like you didn't yourself many years before. Please have faith me in me I can do this Moonbeam". She agrees by nodding her head with approval. "Good so let's begin"

Chapter 26

THE BIRTH 12ᵀᴴ MARCH BC

Moonbeam is standing there watching her son laying helpless in the sand and not being able to help Seequest this time, she felt hopeless. She also felt sad as when the foals were born she knew that they will grow very quickly because they were magical and will have to produce their own foals soon and when that happens she will have to die! But for now, she is more worried about her son surviving this. Neptune kneels on the wet cold sand and pulls out his small fork, he shakes it and it begins to grow in seconds, it has a bright blue flame sitting on the top of it, he starts to move it around to Seequests stomach it begins to cut his flesh blood starts to seep out slowly all over the beach where the male laid. Neptune carries on and does the procedure again and this time it cuts into the inner part of his belly, gradually his organs pop out over his body, Neptune moves them over carefully not to damage them as he does. He sees the fillies laying quietly in the bags against each other. He pulls them out one by one and then cuts both of their unbiblical cords and then cuts out the Placenta which they were feeding form.

He drags them closer to their father's head and breaks open their bags with his fork so the foals can breathe the Earth air. Moonbeam is helping as mother would do by eating and licking all the blood away and making them clean. Once Neptune has cut away all the parts that are not needed now knowing that Seequest is a stallion, he sews the wounds up with his fork again and starts to put back his organs in the correct place. Once he has done this he begins to seal the inner skin and then the outer skin too. He whistles over to Tidal Wave and Seespray, they ran over to him carrying seawater in their mouths one by one they squirt it all over where Seequest had been cut deeply, within seconds of this happening he begins to heal! The wound had now produced a deep thick scar. Tidal wave (The sea stallion of the two) bends down towards his body and squirts the water closer to the wounds and now the scar is gone as if it never happened. The Seahorse stands again and walks away. The sea god touches the stallion to make sure he is breathing well. He smiles and then commands both horses to gently drag Seequest's body into the sea by his tail. They drag him as far as he can go, just floating in the current until they take him under with them. He is still in this coma sleep knowing nothing that was going on. He was in memory of when his mother was younger and strong. Moonbeam sees this happening and starts to fret and worry for him! But she has faith and hope in Neptune that her son is in great hands of the Gods. As she too was saved by this Merman herself in the past.

Moonbeam looked at the sea. there was no change yet Neptune walks over to Moonbeam and the foals she is licking them thoroughly clean. He hugs her around the neck and says to" please stop worrying girl his alright and after all he now is the king of Unicorns and horses, he can and will do this, believe in him"! He holds her mane and helps feed the foals, he checks them over and knows that they are both healthy, plus you can see they are unicorns as their horns have grown into their foreheads already. He was amazed by these little fillies he says, "you should be proud he has produced to beautiful foals and smiles at her" You are now grandmother Moonbeam, by hearing this frightened her that she was old and nearer to her death then she had thought. They feed the babies with seaweed and sea water as they have the power of the sea and will be the only ones that will ever again. Neptune collected lots more seaweed and pointed his fork into it to create a blanket for the foals to keep warm at night.

The next morning the foals had opened their deep brown eyes, they had the same as Moonbeam so they could live in the day and the night like the horse will one day too. The fillies were so cute there was one pinto/ paint black and white patches and one was a dark bay with black under her eyes and on her muzzle as well has on her mane and tail and black forelocks. Moonbeam gives them Seawater for them to drink from a shell, which turns into milk, she also gives them the nectar from these special flowers which turn into powder and will help them strengthen the flower was called Sweet Heart Drops, it was good for their health as remember they have the power of the Earth unicorns as well. The foals begin to act more lively and energetic, they try and to stand up yet they are still wobbly at this moment and fall straight to the sand with a bash. Neptune laughs and says, "you will get the hang of it, give yourselves time to build your strengths, you remind me of your father when he was a foal". Moonbeam nuzzles them both giving them love and security, she looks at them both and licks their faces one at a time and feels overwhelmed with the love that she has for them. The fillies decide to get up and wobbled a few times and then they managed to straighten their legs right up, within a few minutes they are both standing proud and strong the same time as after all they are twins. They walked over to their nan with ease holding their heads high as they walked to her. That afternoon Moonbeam was laying back down with the foals curled between her. Moonbeam says to them "your father will be here soon", knowing she was worried, because he is not back from the sea yet! Seequest is laying on the bottom of the seabed resting while all his body was collecting its power again and completely healing in every way possible. Neptune knows that his work is done and walks back into the sea to his proper form and swims away.

Within that second a noise appears from the sea, she wakes up with her head and neck laying straight on the sand. She sees an image of something Grey popping out of the sea with a powerful blue horn connected to it, as ✓ it's shadow came closer the horn glowed stronger, she realized it was her son, he was coming home. She could see that Seequest was galloping as fast has he could between the rough waves with the other hippocampus and his friends the dolphins. Galloping nearer and nearer to the beach. It took him a while to get back towards the land as it was windy and the waves were very strong. Another day had passed and its night time the moon was glowing in the water and above like a white opal. It lit up following Seequests movements. He is nearly to the shore at last and canters over to his mother proudness in his eyes seeing that is children are lying beside her peacefully. He stops and rears up with true power of the greatest creature that ever lived on Earth. The foals shook because of the noise and then Seequest realized he had to be different now as he is a father first and needs consider their needs. He nuzzled them both to wake them up and they stood looking at him knowing that he was their father. They neighed with their little voices "fear not my sweet ones I am your father and King of the Unicorns and the Horse.

Moonbeam had already explained a lot to them about their father earlier and that they had his powers from their horns, which they will be taught how to use one day and that they will also grow up fast too like he did as a foal. Moonbeam walks away slowly as she is getting weaker every month. Her coat has turned to blackish grey due to her age with some white patches appearing around eyes; forehead; mouth and legs too. Moonbeam now was getting very old.

Neptune rides out on his sea horses to greet Seequest back to make sure he is alright and to properly introduce themselves to the foals. They all reach the family on the sand and bow down to Seequest, he also bows his head back as respect, Tidal Wave and Seespray bowed. As well. The Unicorn King Shakes his head and neighs at them and closing his eyes. They greet properly afterwards by rubbing their bodies and faces together. The fillies try to do this as well.

Chapter 27

SEEQUEST'S DAUGHTERS

Weeks have passed and the foals are getting stronger every day. He approaches the fillies carefully as he is twice the size of his mother and he did not want to scare them off. He first sees his actual daughter who is a beautiful marked Pinto, her background was white laid neatly over her body and her black patches were nicely positioned too. The filly had black patches softy over her eyes, they were also blue like her father, as they changed from time to time if she was near the sea. Her body build was the same of Moonbeam's, her mane and tail was neatly feathery mixed with both colors black and white and her horn was jet black with silver running through the rims. Her legs had slight black marks on the white too. She was stunning and in the correct sunlight her horn would glisten. She looked up and saw her father standing there watching her, so she walks up to him with grace and tries to rear up and stumbles and lands on her side, she felt foolish and would not look at her father after that. He laughs at her and said, "mother we shall call her Spirit of the Spring, Spirit for short"! Moonbeam neighed with happiness and herself and Spirit was delighted with the name. He saw his other daughter a more broader and taller type with a nice chiseled neck and longer face then the first. This foal was unusual as she had a deep brown coat like Truth with a black mane and tail and black around her eyes and on her legs with Amber eyes hers to could change in the sunlight she had strong white star mark on forehead too like Moonbeam (stunning). Her body build was like a Thoroughbred of today She seemed to be more calmer and had a more relaxed personality than her sister. Seequest says "I will call you The Star of The Sea and Star for short" Her horn was black with a soft amber twirled around like trees of the Earth. Everyone is delighted of by what has just happened as Seequest and Moonbeam knew that this was a onetime Miracle! Seequest feels that someone is approaching and to protect his family runs towards the beach leaving them behind. There appears Neptune, Seequest neighs and runs to him and stops right in front of where he was standing and rears up with joy to see him" Hello my friend your looking better I must say! The King kneels in front of Neptune now in human form and jumps on his back and gallops towards The Woods of Paradise were they all live now until the fillies are stronger. They arrive and Neptune jumps off, Moonbeam is grazing with her granddaughters The Sea God walks up to Moonbeam and strokes her gently" Hello old friend" and senses her pain of old age. Seequest could see in his mother's eyes something was wrong and decided to stand beside her by cuddling her with his whole neck over her showing his love also knowing that he could not help his mother this time round. Neptune says, "well done my lovelies", all the Unicorns neighed together with joy! Moonbeam then called the fillies names when they are standing in front of her she bows before them. The foals nuzzled her with great love. Moonbeam smiled and then turned and smiled at her son. Seequest waved his head up and down with his mane flying everywhere very proud. The foals say hello to Neptune and he has as a good look at them to make sure they are growing and doing well, as remember these were a miracle! Seequest says" my children you are both a miracle, you will know all of the knowledge about Earth. "You my beauties will one day help me to produce the HORSE". The fillies neighed with excitement and then galloped away on their own. As they had grown so much.

Moonbeam pushes her son gently saying" Son I will teach you and your daughters everything I know, Seequest whines and then his eyes began to fill with water. Yet he would not cry in front of his mother. Because he knew from these words that when things are done and ready she will have to leave them for good even the most powerful Unicorn on Earth has his boundaries. Seequest loves his mother very much and yet he cannot save her from the rules of Hades or Earth which is Life & Death. They all soon forget about the sadness which will follow in time. Now they attend to the fillies, Neptune Whispers in Moonbeams ear something and she looks very sad afterwards he kisses her nose and walks away. There standing from nowhere is Tidal wave a Stunning Pure White Stallion with blue eyes neighing at them calling for his master. "Ok boy" Neptune says and jumps on him and gallops back towards the beach and disappears into the sea once more.

Many Months later Seequest thought it was time to introduce the fillies to the beach and specially the sea! Spirit walked straight up to the shore and sniffed the sand and then dived in as she was a natural where Star was unsure, probably because her father is Truth after all and he is an Earth Unicorn, who has never been or touched the sea as it is poisonous to him but because Seequest carried her she has the power like the rest of them of drinking and eating from the sea for strength, healing and energy. Star still is watching Spirit jumping around in the sea and through seeing this she gets excited and runs after her. Later Moonbeam is coaching Star that she is Safe and ok. As she freezes half way in the sea, Moonbeam says "it is alright my darling we all have fears" and eventually Star listens to her grand mare and starts to follow carefully further into the sea, Moonbeam says drink to her and she does not pay attention, as she is too frightened and freezes again where she is. The filly watches Moonbeam drink the seawater and then tries it and spits it out with a horrible expression on her face and she felt that she did not belong there. She turns around and walks back to the shore. Moonbeam feels it for her and goes and comforts her for a while on the soft silky yellow sand. While Spirit and her father are still enjoying themselves in the sea.

A week had pasted and Star had become better with water but was not a lover of it still. She loved to eat and drink from the woods the fruits and streams, which would have been the normal way for an Earth Unicorn to do like her father and drink the Nectar from the pretty flowers for energy instead. Later, that day Seequest requested that everyone has a nice canter on the beach with him like the family they were. After their canter which was breath taking they all laid behind the rocks for safety from predators, as no one knows if the Sabre Tooth Tigers are still on Earth as they have vanished?? Moonbeam tells the fillies about their destiny and why they were born in the first place and why they are very special and different from any of their kind before them. She explained how important they were to create one day a new complete species here on Earth.

Chapter 28

SPIRIT AND STAR ARE
NOW GROWN MARES

Six more months had passed and winter is here. The mares are half the size of Moonbeam and have grown with great speed. Moonbeam tells the fillies that one day they too will become mothers and carry their own children the way it should be done, Moonbeam tells Star that she will mate with Seequest and that Spirit would have to go to the woods and mate with Truth. Even though Seequest had carried them both. Star is still Truth's true off spring. The Unicorn fillies were bred from two different genes and it would not affect the bloodlines because of the magic involved., Once they knew this they would be ok, they then agreed to their destinies. Spirit would bear black and white foals representing Purity, Peace and spirituality and Star would produce bays of solid colors that we know today. They will carry two foals, each one son and one daughter. These creatures will be the first horses on Earth there will be no more Unicorns, as Spirit and Star are the last of them. Once the fillies heard this their heads sunk with sadness. But they knew why as Humans are going to take over the world one day and make it better for everyone hopefully! It was a cold chilly day everyone was enjoying each other's company as usual. Another six months later Star was properly introduced to Seequest as a mare and stallion does and was acquainted to him, as she never felt that he was her true father anyway. Just a dear friend in her eyes. And Moonbeam took Spirit to meet Truth for the first time, she felt unsure of what was going to happen to her. But later she understood what she will do in the future. They were still too young to mate and just getting comfortable for when the time was right later in the future, which will not be long.

They all come together for Spring again and each filly had grown into a beautiful young mare still not able to mate yet though. But the time was getting closer as after all they were magic Unicorns aging fast for survival and to originally always make sure they were enough of their kind to do the work on Earth that Pegasus had put their ancestors there to do nearly a century before them.

Star had grown to be a beautiful strong mare for one so young and loved to run for long distances she also loved jumping too. Her coat had become darker than her father's. Her head and body was covered in muscles in an elegant way all over her neck and shoulders to her withers and back with a shorter and straighter mane and tail, she could jump very high! Star had amber eyes, which would glow in the sunshine and lite the day. Seequest liked the look of this filly as he knew she would produce some great offspring and survive the birth. Seequest decided that he will try to get Star on her own. But she always wanted to stay with Moonbeam, Seequest was getting cross and decided that his mother will tell him when it was time, as his hormones where going crazy because it's just instinct for a stallion to pick his mare months before they mate in the wild and stay together for a while if they can. But she was not having none of it "Leave her" Moonbeam said, so he did. Now Spirit was the complete opposite she seemed to be excited and eager to meet again with her uncle, knowing that he has a special connection with nature, she would visit him a few times while he was still in the Great oak tree in Mysterious Woods. Time was going so fast now it seemed a long time since Spirit and Star was foals. Moonbeam was starting to get really slow as if she had developed arthritis in her legs and her coat had turned to a bluey black through age, her mane and tail was also thinning out due to her age as well. She looked at her granddaughters thinking once she used to look like that and felt a little envious yet still loved them dearly though. She Could not believe her eyes that they had grown into some amazing mares in so little time, their horns were more powerful too, they used to help their father with all the duties he still did knowing that the others were all gone. Spirit used to help keep the sky / stars and Moon healthy while Star helped with the woods; streams and all living creatures. Moonbeam knew the time had come for them to become mothers.

While they are sitting down one night near the beach she tells them what will happen to them while they are pregnant and what to except after the foals were born, she also reassured them that she will be there to help and comfort them too. Seequest is doing his rounds as usual Standing on the cliff top where he can watch the sea and his family all at the same time. Moonbeam calls him he then starts to gallop down like a flash, Star acts a little grumpy as she is just ending her season and would not interact with Seequest. He gets annoyed with her and nips her back to tell her to behave and give him some respect. Through this she soon calms down and listens and obeys as she is mating with the King of Unicorns after all, not just a stallion from a herd. Eventually she accepts and he kisses her face. They gallop off together to the other side of the beach where it was warmer and drier, knowing that she was not a lover of the sea.

Moonbeam tells Spirit it is time and takes her to the Oak tree, she also tells Spirit to use her horn by touching where Truths head is laying and to be patient. Moonbeam smiles and trots off while Spirit lays down after standing for hours for Truth to appear, she's feeling tired now and falls asleep. That night the Oak tree glows and out jumps Truth himself in full form, he wakes her up by standing on his hind's legs neighing at her loudly. Spirit quickly jumps to her feet as she understands about honor more than her sister, I guess from being the King of Unicorns daughter. Truth liked Spirits bubbly personality and she was pretty like her grand mare. They ran for a while to get used to each other and a few days later they locked and mated a couple of times. On the fifth day Truth returned into the tree. Spirit felt relieved and tired so she just slept and ate and drank most of the next few days while she was alone,

While this was happening, Moonbeam had been visiting her dear friends the Wolves Max and Ash and all her forest animal friends too, as she knew it was nearly her time, so she says her goodbyes to them. Moonbeam enjoyed the space for a while. But after a few days she felt lonely and afraid. Luckily the last day had come for her to collect Spirit from the woods and bring her home. She arrived late afternoon with Spirit showing a slight bump already, she touched the tree with her nose and said, "thank you dear cousin", when a pretty peach fruit fell in front of her which an eagle was holding, as if it was a gift from Truth himself. She continued and said, "you will be a great father and a perfect example for this new creation". From that moment Truths head popped out unexcepted has he had a little extra power still and said, "thank you Moonbeam for remembering me and for letting me be part of this new species of ours, bless you and goodbye old friend". They nuzzled and neighed, while Truth and Spirit did their actual goodbyes before they headed back to the beach. Moonbeam knew that Spirit was in foal as her eyes were lite up like stars and she seemed very calm for once," Come my child let me take you back to see your father and sister and they continued to gallop as fast as Moonbeam could cope with, as she could go in the water and relax and feel better later when she arrives home again. They approach the beach and trot down the cliff top beautifully together in sync with their Necks and tails held high as they go.

The sun was dancing with a gorgeous sunset in the sky that evening Star approached the mares with great confidence, wow she had changed to a completely different unicorn that you they had known before. Seequest had made her feel very comfortable in his presence that she now had a crush on him forever and felt like she was his chosen one. Moonbeam also could see that Star was in foal too. The Mares stayed near by Moonbeam and ate and feed with her, while Seequest stayed away with respect and his duty to protect his herd from harm. He had stayed away for a year missing his mother. But knew his duty to his kind.

Chapter 29

THE BIRTH OF THE HORSE

Another Spring was near and Spirit and Star were both heavily pregnant. Neptune popped to see them both and smiled and told Moonbeam they are all fit and well and soon will be ready to give birth to her Great grandchildren and he also told her that this time he will let nature run its course. Moonbeam felt like she was going to faint! Because everything was now happening too quick for her to keep up. The Sea horses kept poking their heads out of the sea, been noisy and to see if the foals were born yet. Moonbeam decides this time that the mares should give birth in the woods as these foals will not be allowed to drink the sea water. As these foals will be a new creation with no magic at all, no horns to be seen anymore and they all will have brown eyes to be able to see day and night clearly all the time.

The mares are walking in the woods towards a pretty riverbank and both fall softly onto the opposite side of it, so they will be together. But plenty of space for them both and Moonbeam can be there for both as well. All the animals and birds had come to watch these beautiful mares give birth to their own babies and how the time had flown by. The mares were now three years old and were safe to be mothers. Spirit's foals took a while to come out. But in the end after her pushing very hard and for long a time they both were born on at night on the 23rd March. She licked them and broke both of their sacs so they could breathe properly. Moonbeam is helping as Spirit is struggling to get her breath. Moonbeam rushes to collect this flower called the Daisy to give her energy and healing like an Earth Unicorn would of have, as she cannot drink or eat anything from the sea until her foals are completely weaned from her first. Spirit's foals were one pure white female like herself and one black male like Seequest's father before him. Spirit had a hard birth because she was a smaller type to her sister and carrying two foals took a lot out of her.

A few weeks later Star foals were born she pushed them out no problem as she was bigger and broader than her sister, Star's foals were born on the 7th April in the morning when the sun was just starting to get hot. Both of her foals were light brown and bay like herself with no markings. Spirit had named her foals Moon dance the white mare after her grand mare. The Black male was called Magician because that was what he was without a horn! Star's foals were called Dreamer as the filly was like her mum, relaxed and the male was called Legacy as that is his destiny! They were weaned on their mother's milk and feed by them for a while. Moonbeam made sure that Seequest knew about their arrivals and collected her granddaughter's food to eat while they were feeding their young on the pretty fresh green warm grass. When the foals were resting, the mares would get up and drink from the river. Later as the foals got older they were introduced to Seequest and was told about Life and death and yet not about magic, as the enchantment was beginning to die out quickly here on Earth as it was not needed anymore. Earth was now nearly ready for Humans to be created and to live there and the Unicorns to eventually disappear from the face of the Earth for good ;(But not forgotten....

Moonbeam was feeling very weak and stayed near the beach now, while all the other horses and their families became individual herds, Seequest would still visit them. But he would always end up at his favourite place where he and his mother used to stay and rest when his mother and himself were younger

Another year had passed and Horses were growing up fast, through having their mothers blood it made them grow quicker than normal and soon it was time to mate these natural Horses again to bring the true Horse to life as their mothers and fathers have no magic powers.

These will be the second generation of the true horse. Moon dance was mated with Legacy and Magician was mated to Dreamer they both carried two more foals each one male and one female. Moon dance and Legacy's foals were born in the summer of 11th July. Their colours were skewbald (brown and white) and a stunning Palomino like the Sun Unicorns before. Their names were called Honor and Destiny and Magician and Dreamer foals were born later that day and were a Chestnut filly with white fetlock and socks and a pretty white blaze across her face called Hope and Saint who was a true Appaloosa of being deep brown apart from a spotted patch on his back. But has he gets older his color will change to deep brown Speckle /spots with a clear white underneath the coat.

Seequest could not live with his original family because they had their own now and he did not want to fight with his own fresh and blood, which were the males. Because they respected the way of the Horse and not the Unicorn, they could not live happily together. Things needed to change so Seequest did not meet the second generation of his children as he was now completely different to them all, as he is bigger and a stronger build with feathered feet like the Friesian and he had a very large powerful horn that could accidentally hurt them. He never met the other Horses as he did not want to scare them or put them in harm's way.

Occasionally Spirit and Star would come and visit their grand mare and their father too and talk about their memories and how the Horses and their new generation was doing. Now I know I did say the horses were not used to the unicorns so too Spirit and Star would go in hiding as they now felt different, which was sad. Seequest decides that it is not fair that this daughters cannot live with their own herds and family, so he says "go into the sea water one last time and tells them to put their horns pointing in the sand and within seconds you could see Tidal Wave and Seespray making the waves as they are galloping and jumping through them and then a large splash of water touches the Unicorns foreheads they feel a tingle and their horns turn to dust and it falls down past their faces into the sea which lights up with a stunning glow in the water and in certain places in the world you could go and see that the magic is still there today. The mares neighed with excitement and sadness at the same time. They looked back to see their reflections that they were now just a horse. Their eyes had changed to brown as well, as now their magic had also died in them, they too could go and live a happy life with their families as a HORSE! When they go back to their herds they will also forget about their father and Moonbeam too until he calls their names. They said their farewells and run away into the forest never to be seen again by Seequest or Moonbeam because they both moved on into different areas and eventually moved and created more Horses. Spirit and Star would outlive their children as they still had the rights of a Unicorn. But their children will naturally die of thirty years old or earlier, due the lives they will lead in the future.

Moonbeam felt honored that she had the opportunity to see them all grow up and to also see what the Horse would look like herself without magic and a horn. She said her farewells and wished them all luck on Earth and felt proud of how she was part of this Amazing Miracle from the beginning. She could not believe that she had so many grandchildren. She began to weep and walked away knowing what was coming next for herself. But she felt that she was ready for it now.

Chapter 30

MOONBEAM AND SEEQUEST'S LAST TIME TOGETHER

Seequest is watching and sees his mother walking slowly to the beach until she collapses on the sand. He neighs from afar and runs as fast as he could to her side. He approaches gently not to alarm her, he nudges her head and whines, she looks at him with sadness. Moonbeam says" It is time my son for me to go", Seequests is neighing and shouting "no you cannot leave not yet please "! Feeling scared and alone for the first time in his life. As he knows his mother as not long to live. He also remembered that he will have to see his daughters one last time to crown them the leaders of their herds. That's why most of the time the mare is the one that will control the herd not the Stallion and the Stallion is the protector of the herd and keeps an eye out like Seequest has done for his own." Come mother you still have some time left get up and enjoy it one last time with me" He drags her softly by her tail into the sea to heal her and to gain her energy, she begins to float and drinks the sea water, she starts to feel more alive and swims further into the sea and it does strengthen her for a while. She starts playing in the sea with her son and he lights up the Ocean with this horn, the sea has become a stunning bright blue as he moves his feet, it shows he is true King of Unicorns and Horses, she loves this magic and feels happy again. Eventually they come out and start to canter on the beach like the old times and then Moonbeam thinks about when she was young and fast like the wind, oh she misses those days. Moonbeam watches the night sky, Seequest is attending to his night duties and she looks at the stars and sees Jecco's star shining brightly to the point that she sees his full image looking at her and hears his voice in her head "my love its time", call him back you are meant to be with me again". She neighed as the cloud covered his image over and then she said, "ok I am ready I will see you soon my love"! But she felt it wasn't quite time yet she waited until Seequest came back and told him that she was going to live out in the mountain where she carried him before all this happened, she felt safe there. Everyday Seequest took her food and she would drink from the stream near the bottom of the mountain so he could see that she was ok and safe and enjoying her last days with happiness.

Chapter 31

THE TIME OF THE UNICORNS WAS DISAPPEARING AND MOONBEAM TOO

The time of the Unicorns reign on the Earth are passing by very quickly now, as all the other forest animals and birds are producing and making the Earth grow on her own,

Seequest had noticed that his mother had not come down form the cave for a couple of days so goes to see her. There she was laying in her favourite spot Seequests speaks to her" please mother get up" as she struggles to open her eyes and will not move. He even pokes her with his horn and yet she still does not budge. Eventually she gets up with wobble and gains her balance soon after, she looks at him and says, "I need to go" with tears rolling down her face, her son nuzzles her and says "let me take you first to see your grandchildren one last time and his horn begins to glow with unusual colour of red "I will take you in the sky, Moonbeam replies "I am not strong enough for this anymore my dear son.

He says, "please trust me". Within that he touches his horn to her chest. A red heart bubble appears in front of her which then covers all her body and it begins to float into the air, she sees everything, Seequest had changed into a daylight unicorn, so he was fine. He took her to see all her family and the herds from a far. They later landed to where her granddaughters Spirit and Star were living now. Whom she loved and adored very much, she walked up to them and they bowed before her and said" thank you for everything you have done for us". He also tells his daughters that their grandmother is a very special type of unicorn and now it is time for her to go back home where she belongs, this terrifies Moonbeam as without her horn this was not possible anymore and her kindred spirit would be nonexistent. Her gran fillies Spirit and Star introduced Moonbeam to their families and to show her how grateful they were to her. The old mare also told her granddaughters to always tell the story of the Horses existence and about the King of the Unicorns who made this Miracle happen in the first place. They then said they're good byes for one last time with their heads touching each other closely broken hearted as they left her.

Seequest could see that his mother was getting weaker and landed her gently on the cliff in front of the beach called the Barracks." The bubble popped and vanished into the air. Moonbeam said "I will be watching over you my dear sweet son "Seequest neighed with fear in his eyes and sadness too with tears falling down his cheeks and onto his nose, which made him shiver inside due to shock. As he maybe the king of unicorns and yet he still has a heart with feelings and emotions." I miss us standing together looking out to the sea, "I will miss you with all my heart and I shall miss you terribly mother". They huddled together and they nuzzled deeply brushing each other's face as they did and then she starts to walk down the pathway towards the beach by herself, while Seequest is watching from above, as she told him he could not go with her this time she had to do this alone. Seequests heart was breaking into so many pieces, knowing that he will miss her like crazy as she was his mentor and his best friend too. His friends the dolphins were jumping in and out of the sea in the pretty moonlight. Moonbeam's coat lit up as if a star was beaming down on her from afar. Moonbeam knew it was time to go has are eyes were changing to white and she could not see properly anymore. After all Moonbeam has lived an actual a century on Earth and saw great and amazing changes while she was there.

Chapter 32

MOONBEAM'S DEATH

Moonbeam is standing in front of the waves splashing her hooves in the water making sounds as she does. Saying she is calling the sea horses to say that she was now ready to be collected. she looks up at her son one more time. Tidal Wave and Seespray come swimming towards her in their Hippocampus form, when they reach the sea surface they turn into horses once more trotting towards the beach looking right at Moonbeam in her eyes. Neptune too has risen on his dolphins in his merman form and says" come on home Moonbeam to me, this is where I gave your life again and this is where it will be taken from you". Within seconds all she could hear is Seequest and Truth neighing and running down together to the beach. Truth says shouting out loud "you cannot go with without saying goodbye as he is getting older too". Eventually he also will disappear for good this time when he goes back to the Oak tree later. Seequest rears with rage and sadness stumping his feet and dragging away the sand towards him. He says "why can I not save you! I am the King of Unicorns

I have powers and yet I cannot stop or prevent from this happening to you" Moonbeam trots up to him and says "my dear wonderful son you cannot help me with this, this is Hades rule on Earth and it must be obeyed with grace. When one dies another will be soon be born or considered to be in the future. That's the wheel of life to bring in stronger and more intelligent creatures then the last that lived before them.

Eventually he calms down and cuddles his mother once more not wanting to let her go!! He puts his horn into the sea and it widens up into two parts. Moonbeam is fascinated. "You can now walk freely feeling no water touching your skin for a while" knowing that the salt water would hurt and burn her because she was old and sensitive the horses bowed to Seequest, they then asked Moonbeam to approach into the sea and they will follow behind her. When they were walking into the pathway that Seequest had made earlier. They walked further to the deeper part of the ocean at this point it came back together and they are swimming holding Moonbeam's mane on each side carefully not to hurt her in anyway because she is scared and afraid but she knows there is no turning back only onwards. When this is happening to her she starts to remember what Jecco said to her earlier, so she is hoping that she will see him again one day, she then comes over sad. The horses speak to her "please don't be scared we are going to escort you to another life from here, please hang on. Tidal Wave and Sees pray and of course Moonbeam are in deep waters now so they change into their proper forms and pull her further into the great depths of the Ocean. Moonbeam was now floating with help of the others. Back at the beach Seequest is neighing deeply in pain. He then hears a voice that he recognized from his dreams a long time ago, it was his father's Jecco. He then sees his image on the cliff top, he turns and runs like a tornado up the cliff path and stands beside the vision of his father shaped by the stars. His father talks him about his mother and what she needed to do was now her destiny and that he had to let her go! This eventually settles him and when Jecco notices that his son is ok and calm again he vanishes back to the sky.

Seequest is concreating on seeing his mother in the sea, within a spilt second, she is gone before his own eyes.

Moonbeam is now becoming very frightened of what to except next, as the sea is getting choppy and strong The Sea horses say" please close your eyes for us and take a huge breath, farewell mother" She closes are eyes and they pull her under the sea to the bottom. Moonbeams mind is flashing all her memories of her with Jecco and her son and his new families and how proud she was of being chosen for this special life. Seconds later she stops breathing and loses conscious, her body starts to sink to the bottom of the ocean. Moonbeam was lying dead like she was in the beginning lifeless at the bottom of the sea. Moonbeam was no more!........

Chapter 33

MOONBEAM'S FATE

Seequest knew his mother was gone and that he had to continue his duties being King he walks back with Truth to the woods where he touched the Oak tree with his horn like before and the hole he made last time reappeared to let Truth back in. Truth Kneeled and said, "my king I thank you for everything you have done for me and your mother and our kind and of course the new generation the Horse"! He straightened himself up and then took a leap and jumped back into the tree. This time there was no shape of Truth. But a shadow of a unicorn left on the oak tree and one day someone form the Human kind if special will be able to see it. Seequest bowed to the tree and "said thank you for believing in me dear cousin and helping me to make this miracle happen as well". Seequest gallops back to the cliff top to see if his mother would appear again soon as maybe Neptune would now make her Hippocampus like his own as that is what he would like to think had happened to her. Days and nights had pasted and still nothing changed. He was now the last of his true kind and felt how his mother did all those years ago and how she coped with the loneness.

Yet under the sea a lot was going on, Neptune wakes up Moonbeam from her death once gain and says, "Moonbeam you are and always will be the Queen of your kind", so you will live with a difference as you will be returning to the stars with Jecco. There you will stay together for entity, so he then puts his fork on her body and she feels unique. As something is growing on her side and she is starting to feel strong and alive again. Neptune then mentions that she and Jecco have been chosen to be the collectors of horses when they die and they will take them onto their other lives elsewhere" "You are the queen of the Spirit horses". She stands up on the seabed breathing somehow with air bubbles coming through her nose and mouth. Neptune touches her again with his hands and says, "you need these to help you". Moonbeam cannot believe her eyes she was growing very large angel swan wings, she notices through a pearly shell. that she is also is jet black and feels greater than ever before. Her body had changed too to a Friesian like her mate as well. She says "I am going home with a great happiness in her heart, knowing this was not possible once upon a time. Neptune says, "goodbye Moonbeam my dear girl, you will go by now as "Celestial Queen of the Heavens". The Sea horses swim to the top seeing her wings getting bigger and broader as she is pulling herself to the surface. She keeps flapping her wings as fast as she could until they produced a whirl wind and large hole appeared in the sea. She takes a massive leap into the night sky once more. But differently this time as with no horn but wings... She is soaring across the sea with wise old owl. She sees Seequest still there laying on the cliff top resting giving up that he would ever see her gain. She neighs and calls him. He thinks his hearing things and ignores her. He feels a strong breeze towards him which wakes him up. He thinks his still dreaming where in the bright Moonlight there seems to be a black winged horse with bright blue shades in her wings mane and tail, her eyes were a soft pearly blue. She decided to fly in front of him calling his name. He did not recognize her now as she was just jet black with no more star on her forehead and she was a heavier build than before. He looks again at the pretty pearl diamond eyes that looked like the moon itself and then noticed an expression he once knew of his mother. She was neighing with joy and lands behind him for a few minutes and folds in her wings." "Look son I am now "Celestial the Queen of The Heavens where one day I will collect the horses when they die", Seequest neighs with delight "Goodbye my son, I love you" "goodbye mother I love you too". She flies off into the Moonlight as she does Pegasus appears, as he has been waiting for her. He is standing on a cloud and then they flew off together in the night sky to the Third Dimension where Jecco was alive and well. Pegasus says "welcome home Celestial and then they were gone from sight.

Chapter 34

THE SPIRIT HORSES OF DEATH AND SEEQUESTS END

They flew higher into the stars where they reached the Third dimension. She landed and could not believe her eyes that Jecco was standing right there in front of her in the flesh with wings too. She neighed with happiness knowing she will miss her son. But she knew they would always be connected somewhere and somehow." Pegasus told Celestial that she and Jecco and others will be staying here in Heaven and this will be the place where souls and spirits of Horses; Humans; Dogs, and Cats will come when they die on Earth later in the future. You will be the messengers and collectors for Heaven itself. You will be remembered in time and through this story that has been written about you and this miracle that happened many centuries before Humans were created on Earth before Christ BC.

Celestial and Jecco were very happy being together again living in the stars with a difference.

Seequest was getting older himself now and had become a darker dapple grey with a dark mane and tail with very pale eyes, his horn was now grey through age too. Seequest did not want to be lonely anymore and felt like there was no use for him so he decided to make an agreement with Neptune that he could say no too. First Seequest went and checked on all the horses and his daughters from afar. Then he went and saw Truth who came out and died with front him being there, his body was turned to ashes and flew into the air so they will land everywhere in countryside, also through his ashes was born mother nature herself who would always protect the Earth from harm from now on. From seeing this and knowing this too he knew he was not needed anymore, so he went to his favourite place the beach Seequest notice the time for magic was now dying out. He wanted to go back to the sea as he always felt that he belonged there, so he went swimming in the waves and became a Hippocampus and stayed that way forever more. His horn vanished into the sea which grew more beautiful whales and creatures that you see today and there is one that has a horn too, I wonder?? Seequest was happy being with his friends the dolphins and the sea horses too. Seequest was fifty and preferred to live out his days with his friends he cared for dearly. He became the Prince of the Sea was once again reborn as a true Hippocampus with large fins and flowing tail. His body he was now an Aqua blue and he looked more fish like as he has scales all over him with Aqua blue eyes as due to living in the sea permanently. They all had jobs to do the sea horses produced some more of their off spring to increase the strength and produce mores waves by galloping through them and protecting the sea from harm. When you see loads of waves coming at you at the seaside and you are lucky and believe in magic you may still see them rushing through the waves in time, as they are visible to certain people. It is called ride of the white horses in folk tales and sailors and fisherman believe to had seen them too. I have seen them, have you??

Chapter 35

THE HORSES NOW REIGN
THE EARTH BC

Because all the Unicorns had now left Earth Mother Nature helped magic live in the lands and the sky, which the Unicorns made happen centuries before.

The first horse to pass was Spirits daughter; s daughter Moon dance, she knew it was time, she walked to the beach and laid down on the wet sand at night looking at the sea. Then from the skies came down Celestial as beautiful as ever glistening between the stars and the moonlight, flapping her wings to land and greets her, she touches her nose and Moon dance closes her eyes and appears her silhouette of her true form, which was her spirit. Celestial flaps her wings faster so that the dust makes the stairway to heaven. She says "it is ok my child you are going home and then Moon dance approaches the stairs to climb the clouds as she does, Celestial blows chilly air onto the shell of her body and it begins to rot slowly. But the rest will be pulled out to sea. Moon dance feels confident and begins to gallop faster up into the sky, Celestial follows behind her until they reach a very bright light which is where Jecco opens the heaven gates and welcomes Moon dance in. They both walk through the light and the gates close and the staircase of clouds is gone from sight.

Is this the end or maybe a new beginning??

The Hippocampus (sea horse's) in time started to change over time to become more fish like and smaller yet they kept a similar head of the horse, yet the father was bigger than the female and carries the babies full term like Seequest did for his family many centuries before. Magic was starting to die in the sea as well, as eventually even the Human's did not believe in Neptune the Sea God anymore and so he to faded away back to Olympus where he probably still is today watching and looking after his creatures from above.

Chapter 36

WHAT HAPPENED MUCH LATER AFTER THE REIGN OF THE UNICORNS, WHICH ALSO HELPED PRODUCE TODAY'S HORSE BREEDS

Many years later the Horse started to produce a lot of Bay's who had lived with humans quite a while this breed was nick named by human's The Chapman horse as used by the hardworking trade man who travelled a lot. This breed was nearly made extinct in the Nineteenth century. Later they were bred with the Arabian lines to improve their shape and elegance and to increase their speed and strength as well. They then became the Cleveland Bay later when they became more popular in York shire. The Queen holds the rights to the breeding standards and kept from going extinct in 1945 after world war 2. She and her husband used to use them a lot for her carriage work in special occasions. The Chapman Horse was quite short in the back with a thick elegant neck with a shaped head like a Thoroughbred with an extra bump on its face line. Their colour is always deep brown to Bay with black markings on face and all legs with black mane and tail. They are very strong and very tough horses. Later they were also introduced to the Spanish Andalusian which give them the form that they are today in 2017. They have become Legends, as they are the oldest English horse breed in the UK today.

Zeus chose the Friesian for his Spiritual horses as they have grace, elegance and great strength, much like his own winged horses before them. These horses are always Jet black with feathered feet with a beautiful expression on their faces. This was thanks to Jecco and his courage that he would live out forever in a Horse form too. But the magic would lay within the horse's personality and nature like they are today. They were also nearly made extinct until 1913 which produced the true breed once more and is now one of them most popular horses all over the world. Maybe this is the reason also why they are used for funerals and special occasions as they have the spirit and soul of the Night Unicorn ancestors. One will never know the truth.

Moonbeam was close to todays breed of the Pure black Arabian with a white star again is rare, as they are generally will have white socks and blaze going down their faces. as I do believe you should be extra special to own one knowing they too are possibly related to the Unicorns ancestor and winged horses as well. They are well known for being sturdy and powerful horses of the desert as they do not need a lot of water and have great speed too. They are very graceful in gait and build. The

Arabian produces most popular colour's. But I not sure about the Palomino and pure white are still rare, these horses are known today as the legends of the sand.

Seequests's breed reminds me of the Lippanzer the amazing dancing horses of Vienna. They are born most of the time black or brown and turn white as they get mature around 5 onwards. It is rare to have a black or brown stay its true color. If it does the dancing school likes to have one like a lucky omen. They are graceful and lovely to look at but larger than the Arabian and a stockier build, it is if they have magic in them as they can fly for fun and dance with elegance and grace. These horses love exercising in the sea too. Another Breed that would have been extinct in world war 2 by the Germans has they tried to kill them off until the French people hid the last of the Spanish Riding School and eventually sneaked them over the broader, they hid them in farmers barns until the war was over. This how the breed is still with us today and famous to us all.

Spirits is probably closest to the todays Quarter horse another strong powerful and fast creature and about the same size of an Arabian as used for loads of different jobs even barrel racing and herding cattle. Another breed would be the free horse is the Mustang who runs free in the hills of Dakota, their used for similar things as very robust and strong horse's if you can catch them and tame them as they have a wonderful free spirit like their ancestors the unicorns.

They also well known for the paint and skewbald colouring. As the Indians called them pintos where they were loyal and faithful friends to their end.

Stars breed resembles the true thoroughbred of the England soil. They are well known all over the world as one of the great race horses of all time. They are generally bays and yet their colours are becoming to be different now in the twentieth first century. These horses are great jumpers and runners. They produced more elegant thoroughbred's in the 18th century by King Louis an accident happened, which the famous Godolphin Arabian mated with his favourite Thoroughbred mare and produced a much faster type called Latheare, Louis loved this horse as he won most of his races for years and helped make our thoroughbred that we know and love today 2017.

Sundance is of course the prettiest of the, all the Palomino, they come in all different shades of light ash, blonde to dark blonde coat and always has a blonde or white mane. Some solid in color and some have the white mark on its legs and face. These were very popular in the 1960's with Champion the Wonder Horse, Ed the talking horse and Trigger the Roy Rogers horse. But they are very popular for their beauty and their stamina.

Epilogue

Some humans may feel a special connection to horses like me, I would like to thank the horse for all its help for being loyal and a faithful friend to us on Earth as they are involved in so many jobs in the world for farmers, Sports and pleasure and much more I have mentioned earlier. We have a lot to thank for from these amazing creatures which was created for our needs, we were blessed with the HORSE!

From this story as become some important and famous breeds that they still carry the magic inside them today.

Examples:

The Thoroughbred, Irish Draught and Chapman Horse (Cleveland Bay) are used for speed, stamina, racing and jumping and sometimes carriage work too. They also used for police work.

The Friesians, Shires, Clydesdales are classed as the heavy horses for the workers who worked extra hard and need a horse that was strong enough and would last. They were also used in battle in the 18th Century due to their weight and strength.

Because of their speed and stamina, the Arabians were used as the horse of the desert as they can go without water for a long time. They are one of the most popular horses in the world loved by famous actors and royalty.

So it maybe that Pegasus and the Unicorns powers do still live in inside our horses today by their speed, wisdom; loyalty; Survival; which lays within their natures and personalities too.

The Explanation of the story

The beauty of the story is Pegasus represents the heavens of peace and happiness and the Unicorns represented Hope; Love and Healing to our lives every day.

We should thank Pegasus and the wonderful Unicorns for this wonderful gift they had left behind to our ancestors' centuries before ourselves., as the horse to us is one of the main important things in our lives. As they too help with jobs still that we cannot do on our own. They also have helped and carried us in the war and risk their lives to save ours. But the greatest that makes me smile is the fun they give to us by being kind and gentle creatures on this Earth and they carry such beauty as well, this is the real reason I love them so much, as they enjoy our company and yet they love their freedom as well.

I thank god for this wonderful creation the Horse, who he has given us a true piece of magic to our hearts forever.

Unicorns are still living around and in us today for the ones who believe in them of course. They help produce love, honor and peace to the world and by us to help and heal others that need it. They also concentrate still looking after nature and the animals like dog and cats as if you remember Celestial and Jecco are the messengers from Heaven itself, who have now produced many more like themselves.

Therefore, Scotland and England carry the unicorn on their royal crests as they represent magic, power and yet grace, love and hope to peace and tranquility to us all.

Well this the end of my story and my explanation to why I wrote it, as unicorns have a very special place in my heart I believe they were very real many centuries before us. And if you still believe in them, this can make them feel real and alive inside you, which can produce their magic of Love; Light; Happiness and Healing to all.

I will let you decide for yourselves if you think this was at all possible once upon a time... I just hope that you enjoyed the story....

9 781524 681586